Girls
of the
Ocean

Girls
of the
Ocean

MANDY MADSON VOISIN

SWEETWATER BOOKS
AN IMPRINT OF CEDAR FORT, INC.
SPRINGVILLE, UTAH

ISBN 13: 978-1-4621-4121-0

Published by Sweetwater Books, an imprint of Cedar Fort, Inc.
2373 W. 700 S., Springville, UT 84663
Distributed by Cedar Fort, Inc., www.cedarfort.com

Library of Congress Control Number: 2022930895

Cover design by Courtney Proby
Cover design © 2022 Cedar Fort, Inc.
Edited and typeset by Valene Wood

Printed in the United States of America

10 9 8 7 6 5 4 3 2 1

Printed on acid-free paper

For Claire and Hazel, my little girls of the ocean.

Other Books by This Author

Star of Deliverance

Darwin may have been quite correct in his theory
that man descended from the apes of the forest, but
surely woman rose from the frothy sea, as resplendent as
Aphrodite on her scalloped chariot.

—Margot Datz, *A Survival Guide for
Landlocked Mermaids*

Prologue

This is the story of a new life.

"Your name is Cass," Mom said as a car pulled up next to us, a beam of light scraping the roof of the camper van. I saw speckles of dust across the squares, a hole in the corner where I imagined dark things crawling out.

"But my name is Ari," I argued, my eyes swollen from lack of sleep. And the tears.

"Shh," she said, looking around the camper, as though anyone but the two of us could hear in the middle of the St. Augustine campground. "You are no longer Ari from Salina, Kansas. I need you to pull that part of you from your brain like this." She pinched two fingers together, holding them to her ear and pretended to pull an invisible string from inside.

I giggled, doing the same, extending my string as far as my small arm would reach.

"Now snip it off." Her free hand became scissors, breaking the string at the lobe of her ear.

"Now what do we do with it?" I asked, imagining my string waving back and forth. An old life. A life that was three. Me and Mom and Daddy in Salina. Our three bedroom house on Oaker Street, close enough to Woodland Hills that I could walk to school with my friend Bea. My white bedspread with a quilt made by Grandma, so soft compared to the squeaky springs of the camper I laid on now. Birthdays and Christmas mornings and family dinners with Pop and Aunt Margo and Cousin Danny. A thousand memories on that string. A whole life.

"What do we do with it now?" I asked again.

"We swallow it," she said, popping hers in her mouth like it was a piece of toast, a handful of popcorn. Not a whole life. She gulped it down, a weak smile in the glow of the moon peeking through the blinds.

I watched my string, nothing but air, and clutched it to me, afraid that if I swallowed it I would never see it again. That it would disappear into my muscles and bones. I wasn't ready to give it up yet.

"I love you, Cassie," Mom said, her arm falling over my waist, her deep breaths filling the camper.

"Cass," I whispered, as the sound of the ocean filled my mind, the gentle waves on the sand my new lullaby. I raised my invisible string to my lips and then released it, imagining it blowing out of the open window, carried out by the sea breeze.

Some days, months, years later, I imagined that maybe the string I was supposed to swallow drowned in the rolling waves instead, caught in a riptide that pulled it under. But that isn't true. You can't bury a whole life.

Old lives can float.

Chapter One

The rain woke me up, pelting on the camper roof like bullets from that video game all the kids played at lunch, skimming the sheet of metal resting between us. Mom always said that when we had enough money we'd move out of the campground. "Buy a house on the beach and have a big closet for all of our towels and blankets. A washing machine so that if you wanted to wear the same thing every day, you could! Just pop it in the washer when you got home from school, let it spin and voila!"

But she had talked about that beach house for so many years that I knew the house with the closets and the washing machine wasn't real. We needed a new roof for the camper before that. Hey—I'd settle for a new lamp above my bunk. It was too much to even think about a phone.

I pulled my hoodie over my head and ran down the metal steps.

"Morning, Hobs," I called over my shoulder at the bony figure beneath a torn canopy, legs crossed on his green camp chair, a cigarette dangling from his lips.

"Miss Classy Cassie. Good morning to ya!" he called out across the campground. "Hey Cass! Where's your Mama? She's been avoiding me all month."

I turned, my feet slipping around my flip-flops on the gravel. "The diner!" I shoved my hands in my front pocket, the rain beginning to come down harder now. "Or at least she better be," I muttered under my breath.

I shivered waiting for the bus to come. Before I moved here I always thought that Florida was sunny all the time, but when it rains, it rains. Sheets of it come down, soaking everything in sight. When it's hurricane season it gets even worse. The streets are swollen with it.

"Hey," Ralph said, swinging the bus door open for me. A couple tourists with backpacks ran toward it, waving their arms.

"Sup," I said, swiping my card before walking to my seat. Third from the back, close to the door.

Ralph took off as I looked out the window, drops of rain racing down the sides of it. If the bus could sweat, it would look just like this.

Through the gaps in the houses and hotels and restaurants I could just make out the beach. White-capped waves thundered down on the sand, the water absorbing the rain so much easier than the land. "Everything returns to itself again," Mom had said once. "The earth, the sky, the rain. It just circles back, again and again. The water that you're drinking? It's the same water dinosaurs drank. The amount of water in the world never changes."

"Your stop, Cass!" Ralph yelled.

"Thank you!"

I ran down the steps and paused at the stop, looking both ways before running across the highway to The Waffle Stop.

I could see Mom through the window and exhaled with relief. Her hair fell nearly to the back of her knees, braided with a pink and purple scarf. She was taking someone's order, but she grinned and stuck out her tongue at me when she caught a glimpse of my face through the glass.

The familiar smell greeted me as I let myself in the back door. Stale coffee and syrup, and today—a hint of wetness thanks to the rain. I punched my number into the keypad in the back, yanking an apron over my head. Megan stood sleepily by the sink, perking up when I came in.

"Oh good, you're here. I'm in full zombie mode."

I looked at the tubs full of unwashed dishes, white mugs with lipstick stains on the rims, forks and knives tangled up with each other, and always, the sticky syrup coating resting on every surface. After two years of washing dishes, the smell of maple syrup still made me gag.

"Busy night?"

"No, short-staffed." She smiled weakly. "Sorry."

"No worries." I pulled on a pair of long green gloves, my wet feet mixing with the dirt on the floor. "I'll get 'em done."

"I know," she said, brushing her black and pink bangs to the side of her face for what I imagined was the one hundredth time that day. "You always do."

She yawned, chewing on the yawn a little when she was done and pulled off her apron. She had a two-year-old at home that slept at a neighbor's while she worked. I imagined Megan passing out on the couch while her daughter ran circles around her head or Megan falling asleep at the park while pushing her daughter on the swings.

I piled the dishes onto the brown plastic rack and pushed them down the line. Rinse, sanitize, steam. So familiar by now I could do it in my sleep.

When Mom asked Shara if I could spend my mornings before school at the diner, she was uncomfortable with it because of my age. But Mom promised I would sit at the prep table and do homework the whole time. "I just don't want her all by herself," she begged. "She spends too much time alone."

But since I always did my homework after school, I began helping where I could. Sweeping the back tile, color-coordinating the schedule on the wall, and helping with the dishes when Megan or whoever was on clean-up was slow. Eventually Shara hired me, but not officially, paying me $40 a week under the table for the hours I worked before school.

"Baby," Mom said, bounding through the kitchen door with her arms outstretched. "Glad you made it with this soupy mess outside!" She hugged me from behind as I held my gloves out, drops of water falling from the tips.

"Hey, Mama. How was your night?"

She sighed, leaning back against the counter. "Oh, you know. Tips weren't great. But the people I met were extraordinary. One of them sells pans for a living. Can you imagine? He drives in his car Monday through Saturday and just, sells pots and pans to people door to door. What an amusing life! I can't imagine the people he must meet! And this woman I met has identical twin boys. And now they're both off to different colleges living with different roommates for the first time in their life. Can you imagine? Your whole life you live with someone and one day poof! They're in a different state, and there's a stranger in your room!"

"Mom, you forgot to pay Hobby rent."

"Did I? It's still October, isn't it?"

"It's November 23rd."

She giggled. "Oh I'll stop by the old man's truck on my way home. Sixty dollars a month. You'd think it was a million." Walking toward the back door, she asked suddenly, "Did you see any boats out today?" She stared out the small window, fogged up from the rain.

"I forgot to check."

She slid her hand down the door, rocking back and forth on her heels. I couldn't see her face, but I knew what it looked like. I'd seen it a hundred times. Her eyes closed tightly, her lower lip open, like she was dreaming while awake. Often she would sigh at the end of one of these episodes, but occasionally, she would drop everything. I studied her carefully, the hose in one hand, mindlessly rinsing dishes. Her head whirled around as she turned suddenly, throwing her apron in a pile on the floor and fumbling for her purse on the hook.

"Sign me out, will you Cassie?" she yelled over her shoulder, "Tell Shara I've got to take care of something."

I pulled my gloves off as fast as I could, racing for the back door. "Mom, no! You left early last week! Mom!" But she was gone, running right across the highway in her yellow diner dress, the scarf from her hair dragging across the wet pavement before I could stop her.

"Mom!" I yelled into the rainy morning, a drop of water falling directly on my nose as I watched her disappear behind the rows of gray apartment buildings. Shara was going to fire her for this one. Her shift wasn't over for two hours. Unless . . .

I ran to the phone on the wall, punching in Hailey's cell number, relief washed over me when she picked up. "Haiz, it's me."

"I know. I have you programmed as Waffle Girl in my phone. What's up?"

"I need you to have your mom excuse me from my first period this morning." I thanked the stars that my mom signed the paper allowing Mrs. Pederson to be my emergency contact and the only other adult able to excuse me from my classes. I was getting tired of having to pretend to call myself. Mimicking my mom was one of my special talents, but I didn't exactly feel good about doing it.

"Again? Cass, she won't do it. She barely would the last time. Why can't your mom do it?"

"You know why," I said, frustration welling in me. "She doesn't have a phone." *Or any concept that my school might care where I am. Or any idea that when she disappeared like she just did, someone has to pick up the pieces.*

Hailey sighed. "Mom, Cass needs you to call and excuse her from her first period so she can finish her mom's shift at the Waff Stop."

I could hear Mrs. Pederson on the other end, "Hailey, no! I cannot in good conscience . . . "

The back door swung open. "Haiz, I gotta go," I said. "Tell her I owe you big time. Tell her I'll babysit for free for a month. Gotta go."

Shara walked through the door, pulling a pink windbreaker off to reveal a blazer that was too tight on her and black, fitted pants. I worried if I stood there too long, a button would bust off it and hit me in the eye.

"Good morning." She took off her glasses to dry them off. "Cats and dogs out there." She paused at the time tracker, punching in her code.

She walked over to the kitchen door. "Cass, where's your mother?" Shara cupped her hands around the sides of the glass so she could see out through the dark glass. "I don't see her on the floor."

"I— She—"

She turned around, rolling her eyes. "Let me guess. She ran off early. Something or other about a thing she forgot to do."

"Yes, but I made arrangements to—"

"Grab a uniform," she ordered, raising her hands in the air. "Put it on, get to work. Those tables don't wait themselves."

I pulled a spare uniform from a shelf in the entryway. Made for a larger woman, it drowned me, even though I was pretty big for my age.

"I'm so sorry. I don't know what happened. I'll cover the rest of her shift," I said, yanking my hoodie off and pulling the yellow dress over my T-shirt.

"Your mother is an odd duck," she called out to me before I left the kitchen. "Odd, odd, odd."

Yes, I thought bitterly, straightening my back as I got to the first table, a couple angrily waving me over to refill their coffee. *I know.*

Chapter Two

“I've got to come up with some new content. What is every other YouTuber doing? I'll do the opposite of that.”

Hailey bounced a ball off her bedroom wall, her feet tapping against it with perfectly pointed toes. She quit ballet this year after dancing since she was four. There were pictures of her in sparkly tutus and red lipstick all over the house in tiny frames. Her mother had just ordered her point shoes for this year when she decided she wanted to follow her dreams of becoming a YouTube star instead. But even if she didn't want to dance anymore, you couldn't take the dancer out of her. Slender arms and feet and hands, long hair always slicked back, even her nose was long and skinny.

I looked at her over my math homework. “You could always interview cool people like Iziza does.” Iziza was the coolest YouTuber we followed, from some tiny town in Minnesota. “If she can find people there, imagine who you could talk to in St. Augustine. I mean, all of the tourists alone.”

“It's not enough though! I mean, I'm starting out here. I need catchy stuff. Something to really wow people. Maybe ‘How to get your crush to notice you’. Something like that. I could get Kellen to help me probably.”

“Kellen has swim practice all the time,” I reminded her, though the thought of working with him in any way outside of school sent a ripple down my spine. I loved that I knew he had swim practice. We'd only spoken a couple times before when our paths crossed at Hailey's house. Both times I couldn't move my tongue, my brain frozen too—a freaking ice age going on inside my body at the exact moment I needed it to be spring. He probably texted and snapped more friends hourly than I had my entire life. But thanks to Hailey, I *knew* about him. All about him.

"He kind of owes me. We've been friends forever. Well, our parents at least," Hailey said. "Maybe I'll have my mom invite them over for dinner so he'll be forced to help. He would for sure help me get more followers. Especially if I could make him a regular. Girls will do anything for a dark-haired guy with chiseled muscles."

I looked around her room, picturing Kellen's muscles and wondering what I might do if I was as free as Hailey. She didn't have to worry about missing school to cover her mom's shift. She had a closet full of clothes, a phone, even her dad's old work laptop so she could work on her videos. Parents who actually had friends and invited them over for dinner in a house where they cooked food in their oven and the grill out back. Parents who had bank accounts, not a mason jar in the back of the cupboard. Parents who drove cars and went on dates and grounded their kids and checked their report cards.

There were two knocks at her door and her mother opened it carefully, peeking her head in. "Hey girls." She wore jeans and a floral T-shirt, her highlighted, curly hair cut bluntly at her cheeks. "You brainstorming together?"

Hailey flipped around to her stomach, her feet still pulled into a perfect arch. "Yeah we're working, Mom."

"I see that Cass is working. You, not so much."

Hailey rolled her eyes. "I *am* working. Brainstorming is the definition of work. Using your brain."

Mrs. Pederson nodded in amusement. "Hey, I was wondering if I could steal Cass for just a minute."

My back straightened. "Is everything all right?"

She shrugged, tucking her hands into her back pockets. "It's fine. Everything is fine, I just wanted to talk to you about something."

"Fine," Hailey said. I could tell by her lack of curiosity that she knew what her mom wanted to speak to me about. "But Mom! I need you to invite Kellen's parents over for dinner this week. I need his help with a YouTube video. And we need to make enough for Cass because she's my cameraman."

I stood, folding my math book. "You make it sound like I eat so much."

"We could definitely do that," Mrs. Pederson said. "Just promise me you won't pester him too much. Poor boy is so shy."

"And so hot!" Hailey called out before Mrs. Pederson shut the door behind us. She laughed lightly, walking toward the kitchen.

"Cass, honey, why don't you take a seat?"

I perched on one of the wooden barstools as Mrs. Pederson pulled out a glass from the shelf, pouring me some water and pushing a bag of chips towards me.

"Honey, we need to talk about what happened this morning."

I swallowed, staring at the glass of water. "I called the school to excuse you because I didn't want you to get in trouble, but I can't do it anymore. You shouldn't be missing school to cover your mom's shifts. It's not right. You're a *kid*. You should be in class worrying about kid stuff."

I kept my eyes on the glass, but nodded. "I know."

"Is there something you want to tell me?" she asked. "Is everything okay at home? How's your mom doing? Are you guys getting by?"

When I didn't say anything, she kept going. "I only ask because I love you, Cass. I care about you and Hailey does too, and she's worried."

I shrugged. "Things are about the same as always," I said. And by that, I meant that they were as bad as always. That Mom worked all night, slept while I was at school, and in the evenings went swimming in the ocean. She came home almost every night drenched from head to toe, smelling like sand and saltwater. We had a dinner of oatmeal or mac and cheese before she would head out for her shift at the diner and I would read an hour or two before bed, locking the rickety door of the camper as if it could actually protect me and ignoring the spiders that waltzed across the walls as I brushed my teeth at the kitchenette sink.

"I won't ask you to do that again," I said, avoiding her question. "I'm sorry I put you in that position." I felt a lump rise in my throat, though I wasn't sure what it was doing there. "I just didn't know what else to do."

She walked around the kitchen counter and wrapped her arms around me, the soft scent of her mom-body enveloping me. She smelled like Bath and Body Works Country Apple, from the lotion bottles stowed all over her house and car. I even saw one once in the side of the refrigerator door right next to the ketchup and pickles. "You know you can talk to me about anything. I'm here for you."

"Thank you," I whispered before she released me, quickly wiping a tear from her eye. Why would she be crying?

"Next time your mom leaves her shift and you're going to miss school, you give your manager at work my number, okay? I'll figure it out for you."

I nodded numbly, knowing there was no way I would have Mrs. Pederson talk to Shara. She'd fire us both, me *and* my mom for the embarrassment of a phone call like that.

"Thank you," I repeated.

"Okay. Well, I'm going to let you get back to Haiz and her video career. You know, that girl better be able to pay me back someday for all of the money I spent on ballet lessons," she joked as I walked back to Hailey's room, eager to retreat to my math book and Hailey's complaints about her lack of followers.

I shut the door behind me, but Hailey was facetiming her friend Laura from her science class who didn't know me so I gathered my books and backpack and waved goodbye to her. "See you tomorrow!"

I could see Mrs. Pederson in the front yard with Leo and Jasper, Hailey's little brothers, coming home from baseball practice so I ducked out the back door and jumped the fence. I'd finish my homework at the beach.

You can smell the beach before you see it. That's one of my favorite things about it. My nose always catches on first, salt and the sweet smell of the sand hitting before my ears hear the soft lap of the waves. Rhythmic and even, the initial hit of the wave and then the falling back. The air feels heavier too, not in a bad way, but almost like it's happy. The luckiest air particles or oxygen or whatever the air is are just happy to be this close to the beach.

Mom always asks me how things are at my second home when I get back to the camper from Hailey's. I usually have a plate of food for her from Mrs. Pederson, which Mom gratefully eats up, complimenting her cooking and saying she wished she had time to make such nice meals for the two of us. She then asks me about Hailey's brothers, about her father, who does computer programming.

As I stood on the sand, the waves licking my toes, the whole beach spread out in front of me, I thought that if Hailey's home was my second home, the camper wasn't my first.

It's the ocean, I thought, letting the sun warm my face and hands as I closed my eyes, letting my other senses do the talking. *The ocean is my first.*

Mom came home in time for dinner, a string of silver fish tied up with the same purple scarf she had in her hair earlier. She smelled like salt, water dripping down her back, soaking the camper floor that I had just cleaned.

"I brought dinner!"

"I already ate," I said, glancing up at her from my math homework. "And if you cook those in here, it's going to stink for a week."

"Stink? Perfume the air, you mean," she laughed. "These pretty trigger fish are the best smelling fish your smeller ever smelled."

I watched as she expertly skinned them, splaying them open and salting them with the little packets I stole from the Waffle Stop.

"You're so smart, baby," she said, kissing my forehead. "I'm so proud of how hard you work at school."

"At school?" I asked, my voice peppered with anger. "I work hard at everything. Including your job. I work hard at *your* job. Why can't you be like other parents? Why can't you just do your job and I go to school?"

Frustration over the other morning boiled inside of me. "You can't just run out on me like that again. Mrs. Pederson said she wouldn't excuse me anymore for covering your shifts. You can't do it again!"

Mom sighed, standing up to turn the fish over as waves of smoke began to tinge the air. The camper had absorbed so many smells over the past five years that I imagined it had layers of grease, smoke, and grime coating its walls like paint. No matter how many times I aired the place out, how many air fresheners I bought with my work money we could never truly rid ourselves of it. Even my clothes smelled smoky or fishy out in the open air.

"I'm so sorry about that, baby. You're right. It wasn't fair. I just—"

"What?" I demanded. "You just 'had something you forgot to do?'" I made air quotes. "Why can't that wait? Why can't you take care of your job for once! Shara's going to fire you. And then what will we do?"

Mom looked down at the fish, shaking her head. "Honey, I don't know what to tell you other than that it was important." She came to the dinette. "Believe me when I say that I do not mean to put you in those difficult situations. But sometimes, they just kind of happen and I have to do my best."

"But where are you going?" I asked, so angry now I pushed her hand away from me. "Where? Tell me. Do you owe someone money? Are you in trouble, Mom? Where are you going? *Where?*"

"I—" She paused. "I can't tell you, but I promise, it's important. It's—"

"More important than me? Your only family?" I felt my lower lip tremble but refused to give in to my tears. "More important than your only child? This has gone on for years, Mom! It has to stop! Or I'm out of here!"

I grabbed my library book from the dinette and flung open the camper door, running out into the dusky night.

Mosquitos danced around the light outside, pockets of bugs in every lantern at the park. Hobby waved at me through his window blinds but I ignored him.

"Cass!" Mom called after me. "Cass, baby! Come talk to me!"

But I was gone, running as fast as I could, ducking under the twisted fence of the park and down to the beach. My anger felt like a flame inside of me, so bright, so white-hot that the only way I could cool it down was by dousing myself in water.

Chapter Three

I pulled my sweatshirt over my head and kicked my flip-flops across the sand. The library book I was almost finished with fell, its pages splayed open as I ran into the water, kicking my feet up high until I was deep enough, and then dove headfirst into the dark waves.

The sun had just gone down but its rays were still alive and well, spreading warmth across the ocean tips, more dusk than sunset but almost just as beautiful. I wore gym shorts and a T-shirt, both of them clinging to me as I paddled deeper into the waves.

I pumped my arms, kicking against the current, pushing farther, farther than I normally swim, deeper into the center of the waves. I could hear nothing but the sound of my own heartbeat, the blood pumping in my ears furiously.

She can't even tell me where she goes, I thought, frustration seeping through my muscles as I pushed farther, deeper. *She makes me do adult things, but still treats me like a child.*

A large wave approached and I dove into it, my hands out straight. I thought of Mrs. Pederson telling me she couldn't call for me anymore, Hailey having no idea what my real life was like, never coming to the camper, never wanting to since the one time she did she complained that it smelled. "Are your neighbors all creeps or just poor?" she'd asked.

I thought of my mom lying next to me on the bunk before she left for work so many nights, of me asking where my father was. Why he was no longer around. Why we left Salina. To which she always made up something new. "He wanted to sell you to a zoo and I wouldn't let him." "He wouldn't let us go to the beach." "He was tired of listening to my stories."

And that, I thought, as I plunged into another wave, my anger raining down on me so hard now I thought I might drown in it. *That was the truest answer of all. He was tired of you, Mom. And so am I.*

I took a deep breath, clutching my arms to my sides and screamed into the ocean, anger so full I could combust. Suddenly my body seized, a sharp shiver racing through me like a sweep of lightning. I tried to move my head, my arms, but could not. Fear replaced whatever anger I felt before.

And my legs. I felt something happening to my muscles, limbs elongating, stretching, like someone was pulling my toes as hard as they could, another pulling my waist. An internal tug-of-war, painful, sharp, and throughout my body. I gasped in pain but my mouth was under water, yet somehow I didn't swallow the buckets of ocean that should have filled my lungs. I breathed it in, which was maybe more terrifying than the muscle cramp—the enormous ache in my leg that was seething, writhing—and then nothing.

I rose up from a wave, taking a deep breath at the surface, consciousness seeming to return for the first time in minutes. Had I been drowning?

I turned around, the lights of the campground and the rest of St. Augustine so far away now they looked like distant stars, as far from me as the fiery planets were from earth. "Help!" I cried weakly, struggling to swim, when my legs felt like they were plastered together, no feeling in them at all. "Help."

My arms paddled out, one and then another, struggling as I propelled forward. Which is when I realized how fast I was going back to the light. My legs seemed to move on their own. Bound together, they moved like a motor through the ocean, fluid and even.

I made it almost to the beach in no time and bobbed in the water, tears falling down my face. Shock raced through me as I reached for my legs, or what once were my legs but now, were a sleek, almost slimy surface, thick and wet.

I looked down, trying to see them, but it was dark now, the night consuming the water so that all I could see were the lights of the campground.

"Cass!" I could hear my mother calling for me, pacing back and forth on the beach. "Cassie?"

I swam forward, legs still numb toward her. "Mom!" I cried. My arms hit the sand and as I knelt in the shallow water I felt another surge, not quite as strong as the first, lasting just seconds before my legs collapsed weakly beneath me. I struggled to stand and once I did, they felt like jelly, quivering as I ran across the sand, collapsing into my mom's arms.

"Are you okay?" she asked me, cradling my head and pulling it close to her own. "You were out so deep!"

I sobbed into her. I couldn't breathe, my heart pulsing in my throat. "I don't—I can't—"

I sat back in the sand, which is when I realized that I was not wearing any pants. My underwear, the frayed gray pair I'd had since I was nine were missing as well. I was naked from the waist down.

"What the!" I yelled, tugging my T-shirt down to cover my butt. "Mom! What in the world—"

"It's okay honey," she said calmly, pulling her T-shirt over her head, revealing a straggly looking bra, wire poking out of the sides. "Pull this on over your legs."

I let her wiggle her shirt over my butt, holding it tightly around me as I swiveled my head, searching the beach for anyone who might have seen. "I don't know what happened. I was wearing them when I went in and then they must have fallen off. I don't know—I'm so confused. And—" I paused, hearing an audible rumble barrel through my stomach. "I'm starving." I was surprised by that addition. I'd had two sandwiches before Mom came home, but I was famished, hungrier—I'm certain—than I've ever been in my life.

My hair was plastered to my face and I grabbed my library book, searching the sand for my flip-flops. "I've got them," my mom said. "I gathered your things while you were in the water. You really scared me you know."

We walked up to the camper as I clutched the T-shirt at my waist. "Sorry. I didn't mean to go out that far. I was just so mad, and so I kept swimming and before I knew it I was—" I paused. I was what? Seizing in the water? Drowning? How did I explain that my legs felt like they were being stretched like a piece of taffy? That I swam faster than I thought humanly possible back to her? How did I explain the terror, the feel of my own skin at my waist? And how did I lose my pants?

"We can talk about whatever you want, honey." She kissed my salty scalp. "You can talk to me about anything at all." We paused outside the camper door and she pulled me in for a hug. I felt my legs shake, fatigue and hunger wrestling inside of me. I wasn't sure I had ever been so tired in my life and I wasn't sure what was worse—the sleepiness or the hunger.

"Carmen!" I heard Hobby shout through his screen door. A pot clanged in his RV and he was out the door, swinging his arms as fast as they would carry him to her. "Carmen you owe October rent! And you may as well pay November while you're at it since November's almost past!"

She rolled her eyes. "Hobs, can't you see that we're having a moment here?"

"I'd like a moment," he says. "Heck—I'd love a moment where I didn't have to hound you for rent because you paid on time like the rest of this dump. You know I cut you a deal but I'm not afraid to raise your rent or kick you out of here if you don't start making payment on time."

He caught my eye and his face fell. "Course, thanks to Cass here light-ing this place up, I'd hate to do that. What would we all do without her?"

I smiled, feeling like I might pass out if I didn't get some food. "Thanks, Hobs." I turned, walking into the camper, thick with the smell of fish, and plopped down at the dinette, eating four of the trigger fish Mom had cooked before she was back from paying Hobby.

"You okay, baby?" she asked as I pulled off my wet T-shirt, grabbed a pair of clean underwear, and climbed into my bunk.

"Yeah," I said. "Sorry I yelled at you."

"I'm sorry you had to." She paused at the foot of my bed, her face glowing dimly in the weak light. "You know, I know I'm not like the other parents, and I'm sorry that has been difficult for you. But I love you more than all of them combined. You're my whole world, baby girl."

I smiled weakly, my thoughts already drifting away, sleep washing over me like the waves at the beach tonight.

"It's happening," I heard her say, or at least I think I heard, before I was completely under.

But then everything was dark, and when I woke up the next morning, Mom was gone like usual, the sun was peeking through the tangled blinds at the window and all of it—the entire night, felt like one dark dream.

Chapter Four

"Stand right there," Hailey said, positioning Kellen then running back to me to check the camera. "Okay, a little to the left." He looked nervously at the camera as she ran back to him.

"Cass, talk to me. What's it looking like in there? Good? Are you cutting too much of Kell—I mean, me, off?"

I put my face in the camera viewfinder so Kellen wouldn't see me blush. Since my tongue and brain were having a Siberian ice storm episode, I raised my thumb in response. I was glad I could at least count on my thumb. Good old, trusty thumb.

"Thanks for agreeing to do this by the way," she told him. "I know you're busy with swim, but you're just what my channel needs. Anyway. Do you remember what you're supposed to say?"

"Yeah." His hands fidgeted with his belt loop. "You know, I'm not sure I'm really up for this, Hailey. I thought we were just coming over for dinner. My mom said your dad was going to grill those steaks we had last time . . ."

For the millionth time I wished my hair wasn't so greasy. That I wasn't so big and awkward, long legs and arms, no social skills when it came to talking to boys. Or girls. Or anyone for that matter. Hailey wasn't helping things.

"Come on!" she said. "Please. Please please please please please. Just a tiny shot and we'll be done."

"Hailey, I really—"

"*Please!*"

He sighed. "Okay. Just one time though."

"And then if you could just snap about it later . . ."

"What?"

His face was red now as he scrunched up his eyes. "No. I didn't say I'd do that."

"What? Not cool enough for you? Are you embarrassed to be spending time with me and Cass?"

He looked at me then, for maybe the first time ever. "No," he said. "I'm embarrassed to be saying, 'Want to know how to get your crush to notice you? Follow these tips,' with you and Cass."

I snorted, but something deep within me flickered when he said my name.

"I hope you got that!" Hailey yelled at me. "Was the camera on, Cass? We can edit out everything else."

I looked down at the recorder. "It wasn't on."

Kellen shook his head. "I'm out of here. Sorry, Hailey. I wanted to help, but I didn't know what I was signing up for."

She threw up her arms in frustration. "Are you kidding me right now? You're my best shot at success! Cass, I can't believe you didn't leave it on!"

He was heading for the door now, closer than he had ever been to me, when he turned and said, "Are you staying for dinner?"

I felt my ears get hot, so hot I pulled my hair around them, afraid they would be bright red. "Uh-huh," I mumbled.

"She practically lives here," Hailey said, pulling my arm along with her as we walked down the hall. "And by the way, I'm not letting you off so easy, Kellen. We'll do a second take after dinner."

After Mr. Pederson prayed over the food, we loaded our plates. Flank steak with some kind of green sauce, potato salad, and strawberries. I followed Hailey to the swing set and we perched on the swings to eat while Kellen sat across from us, cross-legged on the grass.

"So how's swim going?" Hailey asked before picking up her entire piece of steak with her fork and ripping it off like a caveman.

"It's good," he said. "Pretty busy but good." He glanced over at his mom who was looking over and waved at him as if to say, "Stay over there and talk to the girls!"

"I'd love to come to one of your matches," Hailey said. "Might be fun for the channel."

He shrugged. "So Cass, I hear you're a pretty good swimmer."

I almost choked on my piece of steak, my surprise inhale trapping a piece in the wrong pipe. I started wheezing as my body fought to get it out, humiliation raining down my cheeks as Hailey stood up and started whacking me on the back.

A brown piece of meat hurtled out of my mouth and onto the grass.

"Geez, Cass, get a grip," Hailey said.

"Sorry," I said after I stopped coughing. I stared at a patch of grass near Kellen. "Who told you I could swim?"

"Miss Kalowski. I guess she watched you in gym. The girl's team is struggling bad, and since we share a bus, we have to stay and watch their away meets after ours and let's just say, it's pretty painful. She suggested I recruit you."

I bit my lip. Miss Kalowski had approached me about it several times and I always came up with an excuse for why I couldn't do it. "I don't have time," "My grades aren't good enough," "I'm not properly trained." But the truth is, there was no way my mom could afford to pay for me to join. They had club fees, needed extras for things like team suits and jackets, and the away meets also cost money. She gave me a breakdown of it one day. Plus, they had practice in the early morning and I'd miss my shift at the Waffle Stop.

"Why would she ask you to recruit her?" Hailey asked, saving me from the embarrassment of a frozen tongue. "Why not ask her herself?"

Kellen looked at me and I bravely let my eyes meet his before retreating back to study the grass, like a turtle escaping back into its shell. "I guess she's tried talking to you about it, but she said I might have a better chance of getting you to do it."

Hailey snorted but looked at me curiously. "I mean, you *are* a good swimmer, Cass. I guess when we go to the beach you can usually go farther than the rest of us, but I didn't know you were *that* good."

I shrugged, mustering up the willpower to say something—anything. "My mom taught me to swim."

Kellen turned around to look at the adults who were finishing their meal. "Why don't you come to one of our practices? We usually do coed once a week. You wouldn't have to do it for sure. You could just see how it goes."

I cupped my hand around my face to shield the sun. I hadn't been swimming since the ocean the other night. I wasn't even sure what happened then, but whatever it was, I seemed to have zero control. What if I had another seizure in the water or whatever that was? Besides, the thought of Kellen seeing me in a swimming suit made my stomach churn.

"I can't really afford to do it," I said suddenly. "Wow, I can't believe I just admitted that." But the other half of the answer felt even more dangerous.

Hailey's shoulders sagged in sympathy. "It's okay, Cass. I'm sure if you really wanted to do it my parents could figure it out. I mean—"

"It's okay." I stood up, collapsing my paper plate in half like a taco. "But thanks for dinner, Haiz. I have to get home. Bye, guys." I began walking across the yard, shouting a quick "Thank you" to Mrs. and Mr. Pederson and tearing through the house and out the front door.

It was hot for November, no clouds in the sky, just a pair of gulls who swooped and danced together, almost perfectly in sync. I wondered if they practiced doing that. If somehow the gulls rehearsed this dance, and when they saw a human, they put on a show for them. I smiled, grateful I was thinking about that instead of what had just happened, the birds flying away from me, disappearing into the overhead sun.

But my thoughts were too loud for anything else. I thought about the time Hailey told me it was annoying that I didn't have a phone like everyone else. "I can't text you whenever I want and tell you to come over. I feel like it's a miracle every time we hang out."

"But we're together all the time," I said blankly. "Almost every day after school I come over."

"Yeah but we actually have to talk at school," she said. "Or else we don't do anything at all."

"Yeah but we always talk at school."

"But—" She'd paused then, obviously frustrated with me. Frustrated with my poorness and my weirdness and my bad clothes and my lack of a phone. "But it's annoying that it doesn't happen the same way it does with everyone else."

I was at the beach now, always here whether I meant to come or not.

"We trade big homes for the beach," I heard Mrs. Pederson say on the phone once. She was talking to her sister from Arkansas, where she grew up. "Of course we could afford something nicer in another place. But we wouldn't be a stone's throw from the beach."

That was Mom's reasoning too, I thought as I took off my flip flops and rolled up my jeans. The reason we left Salina for St. Augustine. Our three-bedroom house with the wood floors and the two bathrooms. It had to be.

I sat down in the sand, my hands cupping handfuls of it, sifting it from one to the other, trying not to let Kellen's voice, his obvious curiosity, from bothering me. Trying to ignore Hailey's nice but condescending offer to have her parents help me out so I could join the swim team. Why had I admitted that to him? Why not say that I didn't really like swimming?

It was private here, the place I always came after Hailey's house. She probably assumed I always went straight home. A stretch of live oaks from across the fence sort of fell over onto the beach stretch, and a small jetty with gravelly rocks kept most people from crossing over. I could see a couple of tourists wandering down the beach through the trees. They were holding hands, her beach hat quivering in the wind, about to blow off. She cupped it quickly with her hand, releasing his when she did. But they didn't come across the rocks or trees.

I pulled a book from my bag, *The Wanderer*. The school librarian Mrs. Keech recommended it for me, but I couldn't concentrate. The sea rolled in, pulling, reaching for me in a way it never had.

The longer I sat on the sand, the thirstier I felt. But it wasn't a thirst for water or a hunger or food. It was unlike anything I'd ever felt before. It was as though the ocean was my heart's desire, begging me to come in. The longer I sat there, the more tingly I began to feel, my body mesmerized by the rhythm of it. The salty taste of it.

"Okay fine," I finally said, standing up, and looking around quickly. I would be smarter this time.

I stripped down to my underwear, reminding myself to use my next check from Shara to get more and left my jeans on a pile right by the water.

The sounds in my head softened, the quiver of muscles too, as I paddled out into the water. Like the water was an angry toddler who'd finally gotten their way.

I pushed against the waves, practicing long strokes, dragging my arms back and using them to propel me forward. The water felt warm here since it was so shallow, a low tide making the beach smaller than it was in the mornings.

I waited for something to happen as the water grew colder. Last time had been terrifying—like something inside of my body was breaking out, emerging from itself. I didn't mean to be here, back in the water, but the hunger, the aching pains I felt sitting on the beach seemed to subside now. Like a piece of my soul was rejoining the rest.

And then I stopped, weaving my hands in and out and floating on my back. I was far enough out that the waves were no longer crashing and heavy, but more like soft ripples cascading across my back.

"Aren't you afraid of sharks?" Hailey had asked me one summer afternoon we had spent at the beach. We had swum out farther than usual with our snorkeling masks but she'd freaked out, worried something would come and eat us and so we'd had to swim back.

I can't remember what I said to her, I thought as I wove my hands in and out, in and out. *But I wasn't afraid, had never been afraid,* I realized. The ocean to some people felt like this deep, frightening secret, but as soon as we moved to Florida, I'd felt right at home.

I closed my eyes, trying to focus, waiting to see if the transformation would happen in the daylight, but nothing happened. The sun was beginning to set now, orange rays streaking the clouds on the horizon. "Wait for it," I thought, "Wait for it."

When nothing happened, I sighed, swimming back to the beach, using the push of the waves to come back in. Then I saw something in the distance that made me stop. To my left was a long tail, emerald green, rising out of the water. Suddenly, it crashed into the surf, leaving a streak of green in my eyes.

I rubbed the salt water from my eyes, the burn beginning as I blinked, searching the waves for signs of the creature, but it was gone.

Chapter Five

"We need to talk about your mother." Shara was here earlier than usual in another too-tight blouse, the spaces between the buttons threatening to burst at any moment. I reminded myself to guard my eyes around her.

"She's here now," I said, waving at the door with a gloved hand. "I saw her just a few minutes ago."

My feet were wet, sliding around the plastic shoes I left in the locker room since the law required I wear closed-toed shoes in the kitchen. Ironic, since the law also required I be at least fourteen to work here, and I'd been here since I was eleven.

"Luis?" The cook was rummaging around the huge silver freezer, murmuring just minutes ago about not having any peaches for the "Georgia Peach pancakes" and why did we keep them on the menu if we didn't have the supplies?

"Yeah, boss?" The bristles of a new mustache were beginning to form above his lip.

"Excuse us for a minute, would you?"

He grunted, closing the door behind him, probably grateful for a smoke break.

"Sit down please, Cass."

I pulled off my green gloves and sat obediently, my eye drifting to the clock on the wall. I was off in ten minutes, had to catch the 7:45 bus to school.

"Cass you know you've been a wonderful employee," she said. "But your mother—not so much."

I opened my mouth to defend her when she held up one finger, closing her eyes, wispy lashes just visible through her glasses. "She was late last night. Not just late but *absent*, for two hours. And when she finally did come in, she was dripping wet, from head to toe. Her hair smelled like . . ." she shuddered, "Seaweed. I hardly wanted her around the customers, but since I was out there myself, taking orders and pouring coffee, I was not going to spend more time out there than I had to. I work all day, Cass. I'm on my feet, I run this place with love, but I'm just a human after all. I can't be pushed much further."

She looked at the door briefly to make sure my mom wasn't coming in.

"It's time for me to let her go, Cass. I just have to. She can't be counted on, and I need someone I can count on."

I felt my heartbeat speed up, frantic and wild. "No—please, she, we, we don't have anything else. Please give her another chance."

Shara rubbed her hands across her belly, smoothing the lines on her shirt. "I have, Cass. I've given her a long string of chances. And do you know why? Why I didn't let her go two years ago when she missed her second shift completely and never so much as called?" She closed her eyes again like she was meditating, her eyelids shiny, covered with a rim of grease. When she finally opened them, she offered me a thin smile. "Because of you. Because you are wonderful. Which is why I am hoping that after I let her go, you will still stay on in the mornings. Perhaps even join us in the afternoons. We could use some help cooking, and we always need someone else to wait tables when things get busy. You'll be fourteen soon. We can put you on the regular payroll. Even give you the chance for a raise."

I licked my lips, "Shara, I—"

"Baby, it's time for you to get off to school!" my mom called, entering the kitchen with an enormous grin, her arms covered in plates, mugs dangling from three of her fingers. "Do you know how brilliant my baby girl is?" She placed the dishes in the tub at the sink. "She is acing all of her classes. Gets perfect scores on her tests. And the librarian knows her by name! Saves her all kinds of special books so she can get them first! She's read nearly every book in that library!"

Shara's eyes met mine. "She's wonderful. There's no denying that." She turned away from my mom, a look of distaste on her face. "Have a good day at school, Cass. I look forward to seeing you tomorrow." She added that last bit pointedly, turning away to waddle into her office.

I stared at my mom, watching her hum as she scraped the plates, stacking them in rows so I wouldn't have to do it. What were we going to do without Mom's job?

"What are you still doing here?" Mom asked. "Oh yes! You need a kiss before you leave." She wrapped me up, apron and all, waving me back and forth before releasing me with a kiss.

Normally I wouldn't let her do it, but today, knowing what was coming for her, I let her hold me a little longer.

"Have a good day, baby."

"You too, Mom," I said, anger and heartbreak swirling inside of me at the same time.

"Twenty views on my post with Kellen," Hailey said at lunch. "Twenty! My *mom* gets more than that. Way more than that on her stupid Instagrams! And no new followers. Not one! It's like . . . if an interview with Kellen, the hottest guy at our school, can't get me even one subscriber, what's the point? I'm over! I'm done with before my channel has ever taken off!" She huffed, breaking off a piece of bread and tossing it to some pigeons pecking stupidly in circles on the cement.

"You're still starting out," I said, even though I felt like throwing my tray of cafeteria food, provided for free as part of the poor kids lunch program, in her face. *My mom is getting fired today,* I thought. *We're going to lose the camper.*

"If you hadn't left so early from our dinner, maybe the show would have turned out better." She raised one eyebrow at me. "He would barely even participate. His mom had to basically force him to do it. And since my mom was filming it, she didn't even have a shot of us together, she kept waving it back and forth like it was not humanly possible for us to share a shot."

I swallowed a piece of iceberg lettuce, doused in watery ranch. "Sorry," I said for the fifth time.

She sighed, stretching her legs out on the metal bench. "It's okay. I'm thinking I need something even bigger to get the channel going. Something really out there, you know?"

"Yeah," I said.

"By the way, Kellen asked about you after you left."

"What?"

"Yeah, he asked me if you hung out there a lot. Then asked if I thought he could convince you to join the swim team. I guess they have this coed relay or something coming up and he really wants you to join because apparently there's not a lot of great girl swimmers on the team."

"Oh," I said, disappointed. "He just asked about swim team?"

"Yeah. What else would he ask about?"

I shrugged, taking a gulp of chocolate milk, folding up the soggy triangle and putting it back on the tray. "I don't know."

"You like him, don't you?"

"Everyone likes him, Hailey."

"True."

She was quiet for a moment, which was weird for Hailey. I looked at her and saw that she was looking at me. "Cass, I need to say something."

"Okay."

"Your shirt and pants totally don't match. Did you get dressed in the dark?" she giggled. "It's kind of cute in a Cass way I guess."

I looked down at my worn teal pants, bunched at the top with a scarf because they were technically Mom's, though she hadn't worn them in a while. I had a light pink T-shirt on with a big 08 painted onto the front, half the 0 starting to flake off.

"Thanks?" I asked.

"You're welcome," she said. "Isn't it nice to have a friend who tells you the truth?"

"Yeah," I said, standing to toss my tray of food in the trash. "It's great."

I didn't go home with Hailey, but I didn't want to go to the camper quite yet since Mom might be asleep. So I walked to the beach with my books, getting a start on my math homework. Only I couldn't focus on my algebra. Thoughts of my mom's kiss that morning, Shara's matter-of-fact, *"I'm destroying your life and I'm sorry, but I have to."* Hailey, moaning about her stupid channel.

I tore a page from my notebook and tried to calculate how much we would need to live on.

$160 a month from The Waffle Stop
-$60 Rent
-$23 for my bus pass.

Mom's was more, but she wouldn't need one anymore.

That left us with $77 a month for food and everything else. Since I had free lunch at school that was one less meal we had to take care of. Maybe Mom could pick up some odd jobs to help with the rest of it.

I laid down on the sand, my head aching, the clouds traveling across the blue sky, racing each other. I blinked once, and the next thing I knew, I was waking up with a mouth full of sand and about eight ant bites all over my legs.

I wiped my mouth and a soft breeze blew through the oaks at my back. It was almost sunset, the water still but creeping higher towards me. Just a few more feet and I would have been woken by the lap of the waves.

In the distance two little boys were playing catch with a football. I could smell something on the grill behind me at the campground. Probably Hobby roasting a hotdog for his dinner.

My hand brushed a loose piece of paper. I had scrawled, "Our Finances," across the top, the number $77 circled a couple times at the bottom.

An ache started inside of me, deep and reaching, too heavy for me to name. I didn't want to go back home and face Mom. She would tell me things would be okay. Perkily tell me she'd find something else! We would be fine! Not to worry!

But she couldn't tell me that, not honestly. Maybe she would find work, but she'd be let go days later when she missed her shift, or went missing, or annoyed the manager or wore the wrong thing.

I put the paper in my bag and kicked off my shoes, wading into the water—dirty and slick with foam. Branches floated here and there, pushed up again and again by the waves and dragged back into the water by their release. *Just like me*, I thought, plowing into the water, raising my head to look at the sky before burrowing back in, deeper and deeper.

Pushed and pulled around by everyone and everything, struggling harder and harder to get back to the surface only to be dragged back down again.

Lost, I thought, briefly, a sob shuttling through my chest. *Forgotten. Alone.*

Chapter Six

It happened differently this time, the change slower, and less painful. Almost like my body was saying, "You, old friend," to the hidden thing inside of it.

I took a deep breath, submerging myself under a wave and yanked off the teal pants, leaving just my underwear as my legs tingled, the painful stretching starting somewhere in my toes.

Everything slowed, suddenly. The clouds above me stopped racing across the sky, the sun hovered, but my heartbeat did the opposite. I felt blood pound in my ears again as the long stretch began, my eyes blacking out—just for a moment before I found myself rising to the surface of the water, gasping for air that tasted new. Not like the air was new exactly, but as though some new part of me was breathing for the first time.

A wave approached me, steady and even, and as I dove to get under it, I felt a new strength, a surge of energy coming from the muscles in my legs. *What is happening*, I thought, as a green fin, like the one I saw just the other day rose directly behind me, so close I could touch it.

"Aughh!" I screamed, plunging into the water, kicking ferociously to get away from it—from whatever that thing was. But as I rose to the surface, the green fin followed, brushing up under me to form a C shape, suspending me in the water.

I reached down for my leg, the same slick feeling as before beginning above my waist, and traced my finger down, down, down, tracing the shape until it rose upward, finally, grasping the emerald fin behind me.

It was mine.

I pinched it, willing myself—urging myself—to wake up, but when it didn't happen. I realized then that I was indeed wet. That my hair was mine, my arms and hands—even the pink 08 shirt I was wearing earlier was still on, plastered against my chest. This was the transformation that had happened before.

"How," I whispered, awe rising in my throat, replacing any sadness that was there before.

Since that first night when I felt a shift, I briefly considered that my legs had transformed from two separate stems of flesh and bones into one single tail, but quickly dismissed it. That would mean I was a mermaid. And mermaids weren't real.

But when I flipped around to swim away and saw the green fin following me, pushing me forward through the water at an accelerated rate, I knew that it was true.

Did this make me a mermaid? Could I possibly be a mermaid?

My arms pushed water aside, a wake forming behind me when I turned around to see my tail pushing through the surf. The water felt warm, so welcoming and free that I dove deeper, seeing how long I could hold my breath before rising back up to the surface. I could go down forever. Down to the very bottom of the ocean until it was so dark that the surface was just a distant dream.

"How?" I said out loud once I got to the top, completely hysterical. Tears ran down my face, but I had a laugh tied up in my chest too. I released it into the sky. It felt so good to laugh, to laugh at the absurdity of this moment that was not real, that could not last.

I would wake up on the sand. This would be over soon. But for now—I felt free.

It began to rain then, a drop falling across my face as I hovered at the surface, my face turned toward the sun that was done hovering and was beginning its descent.

Drops plopped in the water around me, pocking the waves with little plinks, each drop rejoining the vast ocean. I thought of what my mom said about the earth's water being circulated again and again and wondered if that was the same with our bodies. If somehow I had been born with a mermaid's body deep inside a human body and that was why this was happening.

Then I remembered that this was a dream. A long, strange dream that I would soon come out of.

"Cass?" I heard my voice across the beach and stretched my neck up, seeing Hobby pacing the sand. "Cass bug? Come in! Come in from the rain!" He carried a flashlight in one hand, and my backpack in the other.

"She's out there!" he yelled to someone in the campground.

Frantically, I swam toward the beach. I'd get close enough to tell him I was okay, that I was just enjoying my swim.

But then I thought of the teal pants—somewhere, floating in this ocean were the pants I purposely took off. In all of my excitement about my *freaking fin*, I must have let them go.

"Cass!" I heard as I got closer. "Cass, we're going to call someone! We'll get help!"

"I'm right here!" I called out, waving my arms over my head. "I'm all right! I'm right here!"

"Oh Cass!" I heard Hobby exclaim. "Someone get her mother! Where is her damn mother?"

I swam toward them, waiting about twenty feet from the beach. If I got any closer, they'd be sure to see my fin. "I'm okay!" I said, as a wave pushed me forward, my body rolling towards the sand.

"Come in! Come in! There's lightning!" Hobby's knobby knees danced across the beach. "Quick!"

I pinched myself, willing myself to wake up from this bad dream. A small crowd was gathering on the beach. Hobs and Sal and Lars, and the new guy with the trucker hats and a couple tourists.

"I'm fine!" I waved, trying to stand to show them it was me, which is when the second surge happened, a flood of energy racing through my body, and then my knees buckled beneath me, my body so tired I could barely wade through the water. "I'm good!" I called to the people on the beach. "Don't worry about me!"

But Hobs wouldn't give up.

"Just get out of the water, Cassie!" A crack of thunder rumbled across the sky.

I tried to pull my shirt down over my body, but it was already too short—falling just inches below my belly button.

"Cass?" I heard my mom before I saw her, barreling under the broken fence and racing toward me.

She passed the others on the beach and ran to me, kicking her knees up to nearly her chest to move faster. "Oh Cassie, I'm so glad you're safe."

She had something tucked under her arm as she neared me, her face glowing from the newly sunken sun. "Put these on," she whispered, handing me a pair of my old soccer shorts. Shorts I considered donating a few years ago since I didn't wear them anymore. Shorts I never thought I'd be so happy to see.

Her arm rested around me as we walked through the shallow water to the beach, a few tourists now gathered curiously to watch the scene.

"Oh Cass bug, you scared me to death!" Hobby reached for me, pulling me into his scrawny chest, my hands blindly grasping the back of his shirt. "I saw you out here napping and thought, girl deserves a break for everything she puts up with, and how hard she works. But when I came back to check on you, you was gone, and your book bag was just floatin' there. So I thought you was swallowed by a wave. And then I saw that lightnin'."

"I'm fine, Hobs," I said, though I was touched by his concern. "I just went out for a swim. I must've gone too far."

"You're damned right you went out too far!" he squealed. "I got erry-body and their Aunt Pat out here searchin' for ya."

Sal and Lars patted me on the back before ducking back under the fence, the tourists long gone by now, until it was just me and Hobs and my mom.

"Thanks for looking out for my girl, Hobs," Mom said softly. "I sure appreciate it."

A pang of hunger struck through me, almost dropping me to my knees, that were still as weak as before.

"I'm starving."

"I got some dogs," Hobby said, leading me gently up the beach to the fence, and shielding my head as I ducked under. "Lemme get 'em!" He disappeared into his RV as Mom helped me up the front steps.

"Take those off," she motioned to my wet clothes. I pulled them off, not even caring that I was naked, and she helped me pull a dry T-shirt and underwear on, before wrapping me in a blanket.

Hobs knocked on the door. "Got her dogs!"

Mom let him inside, where they both watched me devour three hot dogs, one after another, my body slowly gaining energy with each bite. But this was beginning to feel less like a dream. My body actually was wet, I could taste the smoky sweetness of the hot dogs and I was exhausted, which I don't remember ever being before in my sleep.

"I'm okay you guys," I told them both after I finished the third hot dog, sitting back against the dinette. The truth is, I was still hungry, but I didn't want to say so in front of Hobby. "Just tired."

"I'll let you get some sleep," Hobby said, eyeing the camper, his eyes fixated on the huge pile of dirty towels on the floor under the bunk. "But don't you be scaring me like that again!"

"No, sir."

The door closed behind him, a soft rattling cough following him across the gravel walkway.

Mom took a comb from under the sink and began brushing my hair, starting at the roots and dragging it through my tangled mess one strand at a time as I studied the curtains framing the dinette window, the light above us hurting my eyes.

It's not real, I said to myself. *Wake up, Cass. It's not real.*

"Are you okay, baby?" Mom asked, breaking the silence. "Is there anything you want to talk to me about?"

Yeah, I thought. *I'm a freaking mermaid.*

But I couldn't tell my mom. She had enough to worry about without thinking that her daughter was going completely crazy.

"I'm fine," I said. What was it Hailey always said? That fine actually stood for *Freaked out, Insecure, Neurotic, and Emotional?*

Yeah, that about summed it up.

"Are you sure?" she prodded. "Anything you want to tell me?"

"Nope," I said, wishing she would stop. That time would stop. That I was back in the water, dancing with my fin. That this dream, or whatever was happening, would end.

"I lost my job today," she said absently, setting the comb down and going to sit on the edge of her bunk. "Shara let me go."

And then reality hit. Before everything happened, I was feeling sad. Sad because of Mom, because of what Shara told me this morning, sad because Hailey would never change—would never be the friend I needed her to be.

"I'm so sorry, Mom."

"Oh don't worry about a thing!" she said brightly, but I could sense that even she, the eternal optimist, was worried. "We'll just get a new one! No problem at all."

"It will be okay," I said out loud, to her and to myself. "We'll figure it out."

"We always do," she said with a smile, curling up onto the bed, letting her long hair skim the worn carpet.

As soon as my head hit the pillow, I felt myself being pulled into a deep, dreamless sleep.

Which is how I knew then, the next morning when I woke, that everything that had happened yesterday was real.

All of it was real.

Chapter Seven

Shara nodded at me. That's it. No "hello," or "good morning," or "I'm sorry" when I went in the next morning before school. Mom was gone when I woke up, with a note stuck on the camper door saying that she was off to find a new job and she loved me.

I scrubbed the plates and forks with a vengeance, biting back nausea at the smell of sausage and maple syrup mixed with soap.

It was a good job to have right now. No one talked to me, no one expected anything from me, which gave me some time to think about what was going on.

Fact: Yesterday I went to the beach instead of Hailey's house.

Fact: I fell asleep.

Fact: When I woke up, I went for a swim.

Fact: On said swim, I developed a tail/fin.

But did that make me a mermaid? I thought as I scrubbed a particularly difficult bit of coffee from the bottom of a mug.

"You're not a mermaid," I said out loud to myself.

"Huh?" Luis turned from his plating to look at me. "Did you say something?"

"No!" I said quickly. "Definitely not."

Instead of meeting Hailey at our usual spot at lunch, I went to the library. My initial search of "Mermaid" led me to two books: *September Girls* and *The Waterfire Saga*—neither of which I thought could actually help me with my problem, but which I checked out regardless.

Mrs. Keech grinned as she scanned them for me. "Mermaids, huh? Why the sudden interest?"

I felt my cheeks get hot. "No reason," I shrugged. "I just think they're . . . pretty."

When she wasn't looking, I went to the computers, luckily all six of them were free—a benefit of practically everyone in the school having their own smart phone but me. I sat down and typed a search into Google: mermaids.

The first web page I pulled up read, "A mermaid is a legendary aquatic creature with the head and upper body of a female human and the tail of a fish. They appear in many cultures worldwide, including Europe, Africa, Asia, and the Near East."

I frowned—this was nothing I didn't already know. I'd seen The Little Mermaid. I'd even read books about them before.

I found a couple YouTube videos of people who swore they caught mermaids on tape—but none of them looked the same. Some seemed like large, looming creatures and others tiny and frail. One disturbing image of a skeleton with a fin washed up on the beach was especially freaky.

Everything else I found looked either made up or was based on myths and legends. King Triton. The Greek legend about Alexander the Great's sister Thessaloniki who was turned into a mermaid after her death. When she encountered sailors on any ship she would ask them, "Is King Alexander alive?"

There were some weird paintings and artwork about mermaids too, and a lot of reported sightings. Christopher Columbus wrote that he saw "three female forms" on a voyage, admitting that they were not as beautiful as they'd been represented in the past. A logbook from Blackbeard the pirate said that he sometimes steered his crew away from water that was "enchanted" by merfolk—which he and other members of his crew reported seeing. More sightings were claimed in Vancouver Canada, and another by a Pennsylvania fisherman in the 1800s. But there was nothing valuable to me. I didn't need to know about the history and who claimed they were real. While interesting, it didn't give me the practical information I needed which was: *What the freak to do if you think you've been turned into a mermaid?*

A couple pages deep into my search I found a blog by a guy who called himself "The Mermaid Whisperer." I rolled my eyes at the picture on his sidebar of him rising out of the water, his flabby chest and giant cross tattoo was going to be hard to un-see. "This is a real account," he had written on his sidebar. "I will take this story to my grave."

I leaned in closer to the screen and began to read.

My name is Toby Duynap, and I have been touched by a mermaid. I grew up in Vancouver, but every year growing up I would go fishing with my father. This particular day we were fishing off the coast of Montague Island, "The Land of the Giants," my father said. But it was more like the land of the mermaids, as I would come to see.

It happened like any other day. We dressed in the early morning, taking the boat out to Montague in the hopes of catching something large. But on our drive out there, we experienced some unexpected turbulence. Rough, choppy waves made our boat zig and zag all over the water. Somehow, we must have gotten something stuck in the motor, because I could hear it churning, over and over, sputtering. But my dad wasn't paying attention.

I figured I'd go back to see what the trouble was myself, and while I stood on the back deck, we hit a large wave and I was knocked off the boat, but not before I hit my head on what I believe was the back deck.

Everything went black for me. So black that even now, I can't remember how cold the water was, or being afraid. I don't remember anything but her. The mermaid.

She was older than I expected, with wrinkled arms and short gray hair. She seemed to be wearing a winter coat on top—definitely no seashells to my disappointment (haha)—but seriously, she looked like an ordinary woman. Someone I might have passed in the store and not thought twice. She had a long greenish-grayish tail that came out of the water, split into two at the end just like a mermaid fin.

I opened my eyes once and saw her face as she carried my body across the icy water, her two arms wrapped around my waist as she easily dodged the waves that were beginning to get higher.

The second time I gained consicousness (sp?) she was pulling me up on the island, but instead of having a tail like before, she had legs— skinny, white, that shook in the cold.

"Thank you," I whispered to her. But she just smiled and nodded, not saying a word. She just dove right into the water, and swam away.

My father found me along with a search crew a few hours later. I was on my back on this rocky jetty—still out of it. But this is the weird part. My head was bandaged up. Not with seaweed or anything weird like that, but with a piece of my shirt. I must have been bleeding a lot. Later when they took me to the doctor, they said that if the mermaid or whatever it was (they didn't believe me) hadn't stopped the bleeding I most likely would have died.

No one has believed me that it was a mermaid to this day. Most people say that it was probably just me doing it and forgetting it later. Some think it could have been a hermit that lived on the beach and after I floated there he wrapped up my head. But I know it was the mermaid.

Here's the thing: They say we've only discovered 5% of the ocean. It's still a huge mystery to us. So why couldn't there be mermaids? If it's so unexplored, why not? Maybe they're really good at hiding themselves. Maybe they are really strong. Or maybe they are people as well and just transform.

All I know is that a mermaid saved my life. And I will forever be grateful to her.

I sat back, chills rushing up and down my arms. Sure, this guy was cheesy and weird, but his story seemed so real. If it was true, if mermaids were real—was it possible that there were more of me? That this wasn't a strange, freak thing but something not normal but maybe possible?

I stood up to gather my books when Mrs. Keech startled at her desk. "Cass! What are you still doing here? The bell rang ten minutes ago. You're late!"

"Oh no!" I stood, zipping my backpack up. "I didn't hear it."

"It's okay." She wiped her mouth with a napkin, tossing the wrapper from what must have been a sandwich into the trash beneath her desk. "I'll write you a note. I had no idea you were still in here! You were so quiet."

"Well, I am in a library," I laughed.

I couldn't let go of the feeling that Toby had been telling the truth. If he was right, if we know only 5% about our ocean . . . Then it was possible, right?

"Mrs. Keech?" I heard myself say, as she scribbled a note on a piece of scratch paper.

"Yes?"

"Have you ever . . . believed in something you couldn't see? Like, Santa Claus? Do you ever think that maybe the myth is real?"

She bit her lip, clearly trying not to hurt my feelings. "Are you asking if Santa Claus is real, Cass?"

I shook my head quickly. "No. Not Santa Claus. Just, something like Santa Claus?"

She frowned. "Like God?"

"Umm . . . Not really like God either," I said. God was this big thing—the creator of the whole universe, right? So not really God, although if God invented people, he must have also invented mermaids, and since I fell into that category, maybe that was kind of the same thing.

"I believe," she looked up at the ceiling, blinking into the lights, "I believe that there is a lot that we as humans don't know. I don't know a lot about Santa Claus, or God for that matter," she added, "but I read a lot. And I do know that we don't know it all. If we did, our books would all say the same things. There would be no speculation. But the truth is, a lot of what we say we know is proven wrong by someone else. So I guess that maybe I don't believe in a universal truth. I think that maybe we are all still figuring things out. And that leaves a lot of room for the unexplainable." She studied me, her eyes intently focused. "Does that make sense?"

"Actually, it does."

I set my two library books on her desk since my backpack was too full to carry them. "Are you wondering if mermaids are real?" she joked, handing me the note she'd scrawled to excuse me from being late to science. "Is that why you asked?"

I laughed, a little harder than I should have maybe, praying there was no way she could view my browsing history. "Of course not," I said on my way out the door. "I'm not that dumb."

Chapter Eight

I didn't meet Hailey at our usual spot after school. There was too much I had to figure out. She would probably worry since I didn't see her at lunch either, but she would be fine. She had like, twelve friends besides me, and they always complained that we were always together. Maybe they could help her with her YouTube channel.

The bus seemed to drag on the way home. Stopping at every yellow light, even waiting while the bus driver whose name I didn't know waved some ducks forward to cross. When she stopped at Campbell and 57th, I spilled out with the rest of the kids from the Kipling neighborhood because I couldn't bear to stay a minute longer when the beach was calling.

I started to jog down 57th, my backpack falling heavy against my tail-bone. There was a through street close by that took me to my beach. I could swim faster than I could walk anyway. As for my backpack? I might have to come back for it.

The wind whistled around me as I ran, my name ringing in the breeze. "Cass, Cass, Cass."

I waited for my turn at the crosswalk, my arm beginning to twitch. "Cass! CASS!"

An arm reached for mine, and I whipped around, a lanky body and familiar face staring down at me. "Geez. Did you not hear me calling for you like two blocks back?"

Kellen's chest moved in and out as he rested one arm on his hip, catching his breath.

"No," I said, the signal to walk beeping. We both crossed, the rest of the Kipling kids still a block behind us.

"What are you doing on this bus?" he asked, tightening the straps on his backpack. "I've never seen you on it before."

"That's because I always go home with Hailey," I said casually, surprising myself at how easily the words were coming out. Had the ice age finally thawed? This was weirder than the fin thing. Well, maybe not but close.

"What's so different about today?"

"I uh . . ." I paused. "I don't know. I just felt like mixing things up."

"Okay."

"And I wanted to swim from your beach."

He lit up a little. "You're going to swim? Maybe I'll join you. We didn't have practice today because we had a meet yesterday. And I've been looking forward to seeing if you're as fast as you say you are."

My jaw tightened. There was no way I was going to swim with Kellen. "I, umm . . . I don't have a swimming suit."

He shrugged. "That's okay. It's actually helpful to swim in your regular clothes since they weigh more. We do it all the time to improve our time."

I followed him down the side street that led to the beach, the scent of the ocean hitting me before I could see it. In any other universe, I would die to have Kellen run after me and ask me to swim. Today of all days though, all I wanted was to be alone. "I don't think so . . ." I said as we reached the path that led down to the beach. I could see the waves lap up on the rocks, lazily pulling a few back into the ocean.

He studied his hands. "Look, I'm going to be honest. We really need you for a relay we have coming up. It's a boy-girl race, so we have to pass a ring from boy to girl to boy to girl four times and we only have three girls who qualified. If you don't swim with us, we can't compete. We're out of the race."

We made our way down the rocky ledge that led to Kite Beach, a tiny one known for its big waves and rocky path. Most people didn't come here to swim. They came to watch the waves. And I guess fly kites. But most people weren't me.

"I'm not sure that's a good idea," I said slowly, pushing my hair behind my ears. Two weeks ago I couldn't think of anything more exciting than a private conversation with Kellen. Two weeks ago I don't think he even knew my name. But now, all I wanted was for him to go away.

"Why not? Give me a good reason and I promise I'll stop bugging you about it. Just one good reason."

I studied the waves, imagining myself moving, dancing in them. I wasn't sure how to transform exactly, but I knew it happened when I felt a strong emotion. The first time I'd been angry, and the second time I'd been sad.

"I, uh . . ."

"Are you scared?" he asked, "Of not being good? Because don't be. I've heard you're the fastest by far in our grade. You'll be good enough. And if you're worried about the money, seriously don't. The school has scholarships and stuff."

He sat down on a rock, his white tennis shoes already dusted with sand. "I don't want to go home until I get an answer," he said with a grin.

I scanned the waves, the view much better from here than I remembered. "You know . . ." Something caught my eye then, a flash of light in the distance.

"Did you see that?" I exclaimed, pointing to the spot.

"See what?"

"That flash of light in the water?"

He started snapping a rubber band on his wrist. "Nope. Are you listening to anything I'm saying?"

I stared down at him, shaking my head. "I am, I just . . ."

A woman appeared in the distance, coming up out of the water and swishing her long hair to the side. I saw her pull on a pair of shorts, and then watched her walk up the beach, pushing against the weight of the water. There was no way . . .

"Cass, I think we could make a great team. And you might be wondering why I'm the one asking you about it. Out of everyone. The truth is, I've heard a lot about you. From my parents. Hailey's mom and my mom are really good friends. She said you're really smart and talented, but that things are kind of weird at home. And I—"

The woman was getting closer to the beach now. Far enough down the water that I had to squint, a sudden realization sounding through me. "I have to go," I said, turning on my heels and racing up the rocky path. "Sorry."

"Cass!" he called, "Wait!"

I turned then, so much finally making sense at once. "Things aren't weird at my house. I don't know what you heard, but it's not true." It felt so good for my tongue to be freed from the curse of Kellen.

"Are you saying that's a no?" he called after me. "We really need you!"

I turned. "I don't know what it is. It's an I-don't-know. But I gotta go."

"It's on Saturday!" he called.

My feet hit the concrete so hard as I ran that I felt the pads of my feet ache. Cars whizzed past me. I felt my breath lodge in my throat, sweat dripping into my ear. Never in my life had I run so far.

"Hey, Cassie!" Hobby yelled from his stoop when I entered the campground.

"Hi, Hobs!" I waved back, surprised at my own momentum.

The camper door swung open without me needing the lock which meant one thing—she beat me home. Of course she did.

She swam here.

"Hi, baby!" Mom called from her bunk. "I didn't expect you for a couple hours."

I watched her shift on the bed, wiping her eyes with her palms. "Mom."

"Did you not want to go to Hailey's? I don't blame you. It's hard sometimes to be with the same person every day. She could probably use the break too. It can make your friendship stronger actually, to have some time apart. I—"

"Mom, I know."

She sat up, "Know what?"

I paced the tiny floor of the camper. Six footsteps took me from her bunk to the back sofa. Or what I think used to be a sofa and was now a pile of duct tape and old pillows. Now that she was here, and I was actually talking, I wasn't sure what exactly I knew. I knew I had transformed into a mermaid—or maybe not a mermaid, but I'd grown a fin. I was part fish. As for her? I didn't know a thing. But if what I thought was true, everything in my life had to have an explanation.

"You're a . . ." I began, afraid to say the words out loud. "We're . . ."

Her eyes were intently focused on mine, wider than I'd ever seen them.

"I don't know how to say it!" I exploded. "But I saw you on the beach today. I saw you pull on some shorts. And I think you did that because . . ."

She walked toward me, wrapping me up in her arms as I began to cry. A sudden feeling of loneliness hitting me. She didn't know. It was just me. I was losing my mind.

"We're . . ." I tried again, "We're m—mermaids, aren't we? You are. You have to be." Saying that word aloud, admitting it, felt like an enormous hole filling up.

Everything would make sense. Her disappearing all the time, her odd behavior, her long swims at the beach.

She stepped back to look at me. "We're not mermaids. Mermaids aren't real, Cass."

I felt my body begin to shake. What was happening? I was so certain. What other explanation was there?

"Hey, calm down, sweetheart," she said, pulling me tighter to her. "We're not mermaids. We're something even better."

Chapter Nine

We sat at the dinette, her hands resting on mine. "Mermaid is the name humans came up with to describe us a long time ago, but it's not what we call ourselves. All of that sunning themselves on rocks, brushing their long hair. Don't even get me started on the seashells!" She almost snorted with laughter. "They've got us all wrong. We are so much more than that. We are the quiet heroes of the sea. We are tasked with saving the lives of humans, many of whom used to have this power but then lost it."

She grinned at me, "Cass, you didn't even know it, but you're a force of the sea. You're stronger than any man on the land. You're a superhero. Not a mermaid."

I stared at her, shock rippling down my arms, bumps raising on them. "So you're . . . we're, not mermaids. What are we then exactly? And what do we call it?"

"We're the Girls of the Ocean. I don't know. We've never really come up with a name for ourselves. Maybe we could if we actually decided to get organized like we've been talking about for years, but there's no way that's going to happen. We don't talk nearly enough. It's rare enough to see another girl out there. The ocean's too big and there's not enough of us."

"There's more of us?"

"Of course. No one knows for sure how many." She stopped talking, brushing a tear away from her face. "Oh baby, I'm so happy we can finally talk about this. The other night, I knew that you must have had your first transform but I wanted to give you time to process it before we talked."

"You knew it happened? Why didn't you tell me?" My face felt hot suddenly. It wasn't enough to know now. I should have known before. Years ago.

She sighed, casting a quick glance at the camper door and said softly, "Would you have believed me?"

"Yes—I—"

She raised her eyebrows. "Really?"

I thought back to our fight the other night, right before my first time transforming. I was so angry at her for missing her shifts and demanded she tell me what was going on. If I'd known she was becoming a mer—whatever we were, would I have ever believed her?

"I guess not," I said finally.

"It's what we have to do. It's what my mother did with me too. We can't tell you it's going to happen, or what we are. We just have to wait and let you experience it first, so you actually believe it." She paused, her eyes growing misty. "I wasn't sure it was going to happen for you. So the other night you can't imagine how happy I was when I heard Hobs yelling your name. And when you told me you'd lost your pants, well, I knew then for certain."

"Why wouldn't it happen to me though? I'm your daughter."

She took a deep breath. "Yes, you are. But you are also your father's daughter." I prickled at the mention of my father. We never spoke of him. It surprised me to hear her talk about him at all. "Who is a full-blooded human. And every time your genes are mixed with human blood, your chances of inheriting your power go down significantly. Grammie wasn't even sure I'd change, and with you—well, I didn't know if it would happen at all."

"You mean that Grammie—she's a—"

Mom nodded. "She is."

I shook my head. Grammie was like 75 years old and wore compression socks and oversized T-shirts with flower pots and kittens on them. Once every couple months she would show up here and cook us vienna sausages and macaroni, shooting the breeze with Hobby while we went to school and work. She always roped him into coming over so we could play a game of canasta and took long swims in her swim dress that was so ugly I actually hid it behind one of the camper tires before she left last time so she would be forced to buy a new one.

"It's actually how she met Pop. He was a refugee on a boat from Cuba. When a big wave pulled him off the boat, she swam him to safety. 'Right into the safety of my arms,' she always said."

I shook my head, trying really hard not to imagine my Grammie and Pop sunning themselves on a beach somewhere. I closed my eyes, leaning back against the cushion of the dinette.

I'd seen movies and read books where this happened to people. Someone finds out that their whole life they were something and then one moment changed them and it turned out they weren't what they thought they were. Adopted, a bionic spider, a witch. I'd probably even seen a movie or read a book about mermaids specifically. But reading about it and experiencing it were two very different things.

I was part fish. That was my heritage. My mom, Grammie, probably her mom too were all these . . . Girls of the Ocean. It was scary. Scary that I had been lied to for so long. Scary that my mom had been this *thing* and I had no idea.

When I opened my eyes, Mom was watching me. "It's a lot, I know. But it is also a wonderful gift. You've been born with a purpose. And fulfilling that purpose is beautiful. It's been the best part of my life." She choked up, releasing my hand to wipe some tears with the back of her hand. "Besides having you and watching you grow, it's been the very best part."

I took a breath, the flickering light of the camper kitchen starting to irritate my eyes. "I don't get how it's such a gift. I'm scared that every time I go in the water I'll transform. What if my friends find out? What if someone sees it and they capture me or—" My mind started whirling, every possibility popping into my mind. "What if I get stuck that way? And can't change back?"

She reached for her cup of water, taking a long swig. "Do you know what percentage of your body is water, Cass?"

"Mom, just answer my question."

"No—first, do you know?"

I rolled my eyes. "Sixty percent?" She'd asked me this before.

"As adults, yes," she said. "Fifty to sixty-five. But do you know how much you were as a baby?"

I shook my head.

"Seventy to eighty percent."

"What does that have to do with anything?"

"Just stick with me here," she said. "We don't know a lot about why this happened to the women in our family. Why we transform into part fish when submerged in saltwater. Why our swimming skills are so good that we can pull a 3000-pound boat through the raging waves like it's a child's rubber ducky in the bath. We don't know." She paused. "But I think it has something to do with the water inside of us. Because our water, our fifty to sixty-five percent of water, is saltwater, unlike humans. We are born from the ocean. We belong to it, and it belongs to us. But we also," she continued, "belong to the land. Because as soon as our fins hit the sand—"

"We get our legs back," I said, finally understanding. That explained what had happened the past couple times. "But what if I just want to swim in the water without becoming a fish? Can I stop that? What if me and Hailey," *or Kellen,* I thought, "Are just out there in the ocean and I transform? Should I not do that anymore?"

She shook her head. "You can do it. Think about it, how many times have you and I been swimming together?"

I shrugged. "A lot."

"Your whole childhood. At least three times a week since we got to St. Auggy and you've never seen me change. You can control it, but it takes some practice. I'll show you. We'll do it together."

I slumped back, laying across the dinette bench. "I can't believe I'm a mermaid and you didn't even tell me."

"You're not a mermaid," my mom said sharply.

I peeked my head over the dinette table to see her face. "Sorry," she said. "I just hate that word. I'm nobody's *maid.*"

I started laughing then, I couldn't help it. My shoulders bounced up and down, and my nose tingled. I heard Mom begin to chuckle too, as the light flickered in the kitchen.

"Mom, you're so weird."

"Well now you know why," she grinned.

We slept on the same bunk for the first time in years, our faces pulled together, arms around each other as Mom spoke about her time in the water, when she first found out she was a Girl of the Ocean, recounting the adventures she'd had. I was so tired but wanted to know more so badly that I fought the heaviness in my eyes. I would listen as long as she would talk. It was like I'd had an eye patch on my entire life, and now I could finally see with two of them.

She paused for a long time, and I felt my eyes drift, a shout from across the campground waking me long enough to ask her the question that had been bouncing around in my head since earlier that evening. But maybe, my entire life too and I didn't realize it.

"Did Dad know?" I asked. "About you?"

It was quiet for a long time, the creak of the air conditioner the only sound in or outside the camper. I could hear her heartbeat in the dark, the thump-thump that was always so much slower than mine seemed to be. Finally, she nodded. "Yes, he knew."

She flipped over on her side then, so that her back was toward me, her face looking out at the tiny shack we called our home. "He knew."

"Is that why we left?" I asked, the words feeling brave on my tongue. I thought of that night, six years ago when we slept on this bunk for the first time and we pulled our old lives out of our ears and swallowed them.

"That's another story for another day," she whispered. "But I'll tell you this," she said. "When you grow up and find someone you care about, just remember that love shouldn't be so heavy."

I was quiet after that, we both were. But I could still feel her sadness in the night, like the cry of the wind above the water.

Chapter Ten

"**M**orning, Cass," Shara called to me over the whir of the blender. Luis was tossing all kinds of frozen fruits in there, the ice knocking back and forth from one end to the other.

"Hi, Shara," I said, sending another row of dishes down the line.

"How's your mother holding up?"

I thought of Mom standing waist deep in the water yesterday afternoon. I thought of her excitement when she finally got to tell me this big secret that she'd waited my entire life to spill.

"She's wonderful," I replied. Because that felt like the most honest response.

It was impossible to concentrate at school. All of my proofs in algebra ended with a tail. In science, I couldn't help but wonder where us Girls of the Ocean were classified. Family, genus, species. Were we saltwater humans? Or something else entirely? Would I ever know?

Hailey found me at lunch, tucked into the corner of the cafeteria, my nose buried in one of the mermaid books I borrowed from the library yesterday.

"Where have you been? I was so worried I almost made a trip out to your camper yesterday! And you know that's a huge deal for me because that place creeps me out."

I put the book aside reluctantly and took a bite of mashed potatoes, the watery gravy on top spilling over the edge onto the tray. "Hey, Haiz."

She slumped against the wall, her feet turned out in perfect ballerina form. "My Youtube numbers are dismal, Cass. Pathetic! I'm so embarrassed about it."

I closed my eyes, fighting the urge not to yell at her. I'd just found out I was part fish. A superhero fish of sorts. The last thing I wanted to do was discuss her stupid stats.

"I'm sorry," I said lamely.

"And the most frustrating part?" Her voice rose. "I have no idea what to do next. I mean, nothing I've done so far is working, so do I start from ground zero? Make it some kind of silly channel? If a hot guy like Kellen can't even earn me some hits, I'll never get there on my own."

I sighed. "That's frustrating."

She turned to me. "Where have you been though? Were you sick yesterday? I looked everywhere for you and luckily met up with Laura and her friends so I didn't look like a complete loser. I mean, I still felt like a loser, don't get me wrong, but at least I didn't *look* like one."

"I just had some other stuff to do," I said.

"Well I really need you today. I'm going to the boy's swim meet. Hoping I can get some interviews with the guys after. I have some things I want to trick them into saying so I can cut and paste. It's actually pretty clever if I do say so myself." She dug around her backpack, finally retrieving a piece of paper. "Here it is. Okay, so I am going to read these questions to the guys while you film. She opened her mouth, ready to speak.

"Hailey, I can't go today."

She gave me a wry smile. "Funny, Cass."

"I'm serious, I can't."

"What do you have?" she asked. "You never have anything going on."

"I'm doing something with my mom."

She was going to give me my first lesson. I'd begged her to let me skip school this morning but she said there was no way I could let this new power interfere with my studies. "I let that happen to me and look where I ended up," she said a little sadly, gesturing to the camper. "We may have our own world, but we still live in this one. And this one requires money. And the best way to get there is to get an education."

"You're doing something with your mom," Hailey said flatly. "What? Bussing tables? What am I supposed to do without you? Who will hold the camera? I can't do it with a selfie-stick."

My frustration with her boiled to the surface, like a hot kettle ready to erupt. "It's not all about you, Hailey!" I put my hands over my face, trying to keep myself from saying anything worse.

When I opened my eyes, she was blinking at me, her mouth forming a perfect O.

"Is . . . now a bad time?"

We both looked up to see Kellen standing directly above us, his hands pulled around his backpack straps. The sun coming through the huge windows of the cafeteria sort of formed a halo around his face, making him glimmer a little bit. I felt my tongue tighten up on cue.

"Kellen," Hailey drawled, tucking her head to the side sweetly. "So nice to see you. What are you doing over here? You rarely make the trek to the loser's side of the lunchroom."

He put his hands in his pockets. "I was . . . hoping to talk to you, Cass. About our conversation yesterday."

Hailey whirred around to look at me, her eyebrows narrowed. "You guys talked yesterday?"

Kellen shrugged. "Yeah, Cass came home on my bus." He paused, "Our bus. Anyway, I just wanted to say I'm sorry. I shouldn't have pressured you so much. I just . . ." He shook his head, his long brown hair falling into his eyes before he brushed it back. "I just really like to win. A little too much. My mom said it's something I need to work on, and I just heard you were like, way good. So, I'm sorry. If you want to swim, great. We have a spot for you and we're practicing today. If you can't, I'm sure we'll find someone else to fill the spot."

He looked at me, waiting for a response, but I couldn't move. My body seemed frozen, unable to respond to him. Why didn't I say goodbye properly yesterday? *Oh yeah,* I thought, my brain catching up with the rest of my body. *I was figuring out that my mom is also part fish.*

"'Kay well, I guess I'll go. Sorry about everything, again. Good to see you, Hailey."

He was about ten steps away when I finally got my brain to connect with my tongue. "I'll do it!" I called out to him. Several people around us turned to gawk, probably wondering what Kellen was doing talking to the weird dish washing girl in the first place.

He stepped closer, his face lighting up. "Really?"

"Yeah," I said. "But I can't do it today."

He shook his head back and forth. "That's okay. We'll have one more practice before the relay. This is great news. Thanks, Cass. Really. Let me get your number so I can tell you when practice is."

"She doesn't have a phone," Hailey said quickly.

"Oh." Kellen put his slowly back in his pocket. "Okay. Well, I'll just talk to you at school then."

I nodded, my tongue had reached full speaking capacity.

The bell rang to go to class. "Anything you want to tell me?" Hailey asked, offering me two hands to pull me up.

"Yeah," I said, turning to go to my fourth period music class. "I'm swimming with Kellen's swim team in a relay."

She rolled her eyes. "If I didn't love you so much, I'd totally hate you right now."

"Same with you, Haiz."

"Tip number one, always wear pants that are easy to put back on," Mom said. "Ever wonder why I always wear loose skirts and pants and never jeans or leggings?"

I shook my head.

"Have you ever tried to put wet leggings on wet legs? It's almost impossible. Tip number two, always carry a small carry-all. I like this one." She shimmied down the fanny pack I'd seen her wear my entire life. "It holds my pants and some other useful tools during rescues. *And* it's waterproof!" She unzipped it to reveal a roll of bandage tape, some antibiotic ointment, tweezers, and a mask. "I like to stuff my pants in here, or whatever I was wearing, and it fits better when it's dry."

"What did you do when you had your diner dress on?"

She shrugged. "Who ever said you can't have a fin with one of those dresses? I just kept the whole thing on."

I laughed, thinking of her with a long green fin beneath the yellow diner dresses.

"Now let's swim."

We were at the most private beach she knew of, so littered with sea-weed and broken shells I'd never even seen the place, though it was just a five-minute walk from the campground. She plunged into the waves and I followed behind, swimming out just past a sandbar before she transformed.

It was amazing to watch it happen to someone else. One minute she was in the water before me, her white legs kicking beneath her and the next she was floating on her back, green scales beginning at her waist, and so quickly consuming her legs that it looked effortless, so different from the sparks of pain I felt the first time.

"Can you just think it and it will happen?" I asked, spitting out the water coming into my mouth. It was hard to tread here, the waves bigger than they looked from afar.

"Yes, but it takes practice," she said, reaching for me and holding me completely steady in her arms. I saw her fin move back and forth, holding her in place while she held me.

"I want you to just relax," she said, "Float on your back for a minute and look at the sky."

She supported my back, the way she had done when I first learned to swim, my legs fanning out as my arms pumped like a bird. "Now," she said, "I want you to close your eyes and think of an emotion. Joy, love, sadness—even anger, though I find the positive emotions work better. And I want you to cling to that. Take a deep breath and trap it."

I rolled my eyes. "Seriously, Mom?"

"It works!" she said, blinking back the saltwater on the rim of her eye. "Any emotion, just cling to it."

I thought of Hailey today, trying to think of her face when I told her I couldn't go to the meet. I was frustrated with her. That was an emotion, right? I took a deep breath, trying to focus my annoyance but nothing happened.

I sunk down, pulling away from my mom. Water immediately seeped into my nose and ears. "It didn't work," I sputtered, my muscles already tiring.

"Okay, try again," she said, reaching for my back. "Something positive, if you didn't use that before."

I took a deep breath. "Think of this," Mom offered. "A few years ago you came to me sad because you said you had no friends at school. I told you it was your job to say hello to three new people a day. Not talk to them, just say hello. And do you remember what happened?"

I did.

I said hello to Hailey, the sly, witty girl in my English class. She hung out with her dancer friends, all of them stretching their legs throughout class, waltzing to the whiteboard with turned out toes.

"Hello," she said back to me, class about to start. "You're Cass, right?"

When it was time to choose a partner for a group assignment, Hailey was the first to pick. I was certain she would ask Marlowe or Lucy, but she looked right at me. "I pick Cass," she'd said.

I nearly burst into tears with joy right there. Because when you've been invisible for so long, it feels like fireworks, shooting stars—the whole globe of the world handed to you—when you're finally seen.

I took a deep breath, lodging that feeling, as a spark ran along my spine. The stretching and pulling began, lacing through me, all of the muscles in my lower body melding into one. And when I finished, I could see my mom blinking back tears, saltwater into saltwater.

"That was beautiful," she said softly.

"Now what?" I asked, beaming from pride, so much energy suspended in my body I felt like I could swim a marathon in a minute, my body ready to break through this ocean.

"Now we swim."

Chapter Eleven

It wasn't fair to call it swimming. Swimming is what humans do. Pushing, reaching, fighting against the surface of the water. Humans swim to get through it—to make it to a new shore until they can be on land.

We did not swim so much as dance the next few hours in the water together. And it was as familiar to me as land before. There was no fight through it—no attempt to rise above it before I drowned. There was only the harmony of the waves and the ease of my muscles as they moved through it.

Mom was faster, of course. She was a torpedo in the sea, her body moving so quickly you could almost miss her if you blinked. "That's why they can't get a good shot of us! People want proof that mermaids—whatever they want to call us—exist. And they're never going to get it. Because we are too fast!"

The water was warmer, too. Not unlike the air in Florida in the fall—pleasant, but unremarkable. There was no real temperature to it anymore, even though I knew that it *should* be cold.

"Why is it so warm?" I asked my mom when she paused, waiting for me beneath a stretch of sunlight. It would be sunset soon, and the sky was gathering for a show, clouds drawing in for one last piece of light. "Are we cold-blooded?" I thought of what I'd learned in science about alligators.

Because they can't regulate their own body temperature, they take on the temperature of their surrounding environment.

Mom shrugged. "I don't know. I've tried to research it too. We're not cold-blooded, but we're not warm-blooded, either. Because mammals in the ocean need thick layers of blubber to keep themselves warm. And while I'm not Miss America over here, I'm not exactly blubbery."

She shook her hair out of her eyes as we bobbed, the two of us in the center of the ocean, waves lightly rolling past us. "That was something your father wanted to figure out. He's a scientist, you know."

I tried to hold back my curiosity, worried about scaring her off the way I did last night with my questions about him. It had been six years since we left Salina, and I'd learned more about him in the past twenty-four hours than all six of those years combined.

"How did he find out you're a . . . you know," I asked timidly.

She went under the water then, small bubbles rising to the surface, making me think she was going deeper and deeper until she appeared a couple feet from me and began a slow swim back to shore.

"We were both marine biology majors at the University of Florida. Well, he was taking it seriously and I was just dabbling around in it. To be honest, nothing but the water really drew my attention and sitting in a classroom learning about it was nothing compared to being in the water. Every weekend I made the drive to the beach. I just craved it."

She went back under, arching her back as she rose out of the surface this time, catapulting herself high like a dolphin. I bit my lip in frustration, beginning to feel that Fish Mom was no different than Waitress Mom. Full of excuses, quick to avoid my questions, a tad irresponsible.

When she began talking again, her eyes grew a little sad. "He was the most brilliant in the class and he took a liking to me. I'm not sure what it was. We began studying together. He seemed to think I was smart about the water. I could explain things to him in a way he hadn't seen before. How fish are able to move their bones and muscles through the water, where deep sea fish go to spawn. I recognized all of the fish he showed me, even if I didn't know their names. I'd been looking at them my whole life."

"We began going to the beach together on the weekend. He seemed so thirsty for this world I knew so much about. Most people didn't seem to think I had a lot to offer." I imagined my mom back then. Poor, with bad clothes and that floor length hair. I could see why people didn't think much about her and I felt bad that I had thought that myself, many times.

"I broke a lot of rules I swore I never would with him." The sun was beginning to set behind us now, the surface of the water littered with light. "But I didn't tell him. Until one day, when the two of us were out snorkeling, and I got a call."

She turned to me. "You will recognize the call when you get one. The ocean sends you tremors. It feels a little like," she paused, "Like someone else's heartbeat calling to you. But also like the waves are static." She looked out over the glittering water. "I can't really describe it, but you'll feel it when it happens."

"So I had to choose. Do I answer the call and save the person or people or boat in distress? Or do I keep this secret that I'm sworn to keep to a man who I love, and who loves me too?"

I barely realized we were nearly to the shore until a shock raced down my spine, my legs returning to themselves. I stood, wobbly kneed as my mom transformed. She didn't hand me the shorts yet though, she was still staring out at the beach, watching the white waves fold under themselves and spray the sand.

"What was the call?" I asked her.

"A father and son," she said. "Out fishing when their boat capsized and drug them under. I was lucky I was so close, or it might have been too late."

"And Dad?" I asked.

"He watched it happen. He had all of the equipment, you know. So that night I told him everything. All about the sisterhood. My parents. What I did when I wasn't with him. Why I missed so many classes and dates. Where I went."

"Wow," I said, my fingers moving across the tips of the water, playing the biggest piano in the world.

"He proposed that night." She laughed a little. "He seemed to be the only person in the world who loved me."

"I'm sorry, Mom," I said, even though I wanted to know more. I wanted to know why we left, what changed between them. I wanted to know everything.

She rummaged in her fanny pack, handing me my shorts and pulling her own loose pants over her legs.

"That was fun," she said, breaking out of her trance. "I've loved spending the past few days with you. I've dreamt of them your entire life."

"I've loved it too," I said, and that was the truth. My homework was neglected, I hadn't been to Hailey's for days, we were living off of $160 a month, and still—I was happy.

"Now let's get you some food," she said. "Maybe we can convince Hobby to grill us a burger. I remember what it's like in the beginning. You're starving all the time."

But after Hobby begrudgingly came out of his camper to light the grill and fire up some burgers (I had two), I caught Mom staring off into the ocean. It was dark now, the moon hanging over the water, leaving a bright white spot in the center, no matter where you stood.

And I thought then that it was no wonder I loved the ocean so much. My mom and dad fell in love there.

Kellen found me outside during lunch. Hailey was buried in her phone "blitzing," whatever that was, while I stared at the sky, a slice of bad pizza in my hand. I knew I should be grateful for the free food, since there certainly wasn't enough of it at home, but between the cafeteria lunch and the scraps I brought home from the Waffle Stop, I was craving something real.

"Hey, Cass," he called out, stepping over our backpacks.

Hailey sat up attentively, a grin across her face at the sight of Kellen. "Hey, Cass?" she asked. "Years of friendship, and you say 'Hey, Cass'?" She rolled her eyes and flipped him off.

He shrugged. "Hey, Haiz. What's up?"

I pushed aside my lunch tray, everything on it demolished. The pizza, little container of overcooked broccoli, carton of milk, and banana peel.

"Hey," I said, praying that the ice age was over for good.

"So umm, we have our last practice today before the relay. And I guess it's mandatory. So, I don't know if you have other plans but we—" He bounced from one foot to the other.

"She'll be there!" Hailey said, resting her arm on me. "She wouldn't miss it for the world."

"Thanks, Haiz," I said under my breath. To be honest, I didn't have that much to do this afternoon. Just the usual swim with Mom. But the thought of missing that to swim in a *pool* seemed like such a shame. Still, maybe it would encourage Mom to look for a job while I was gone. Almost two weeks of unemployment and she hadn't had so much as an interview.

"That would be so cool," he said. "It's in the big gym. The one—"

"I know," I said. "I'll be there."

"Cool." He stood there, looking hopefully back at the cafeteria, his friends waving him over between glances at their phones.

"Back to your posse," Hailey shooed him away. When he was out of earshot, she said, "Since when does Kellen actually find us not once, but twice in a week?"

"Since he needs me to win a race."

"I wish I could swim," she said mindlessly, watching him disappear into the lunchroom, flexing her feet in and out and not even realizing she was doing it.

Miss Kalowski nodded approvingly at me as I walked across the pool floor, a towel wrapped around my body even though I wasn't wet yet. I had to borrow one of the swimming suits from the lost and found since I didn't have one, and it wasn't quite long enough for my torso, making it ride up around my cheeks. I knew I had a wedgie. But that was only half the problem.

The other was that there was zero bra support. And while I wasn't exactly gifted in the boob department, I had some small mounds that needed a little care.

"I'm so glad you came out," she said, an echo bouncing off the gym walls. "I knew I could talk all I wanted and, in the end, you'd respond a lot better to Kellen's cute face."

I blushed. "He said they'd be disqualified if I didn't come."

She nodded, scanning the room and waving as the other swimmers came over. "He's right. So this is all we're doing. You get passed a baton— well, a ring, and swim from one end to the other of the pool six times. It has to be that many because for the real thing, we're in the ocean and we don't have a pool big enough to practice on. It will go boy girl boy girl. You'll get —"

"Did you just say the race is in the ocean?" I asked, nerves suddenly raining down on me. The ocean. My ocean.

"Is that a problem?" she asked kindly. "Honey, if you're afraid of sharks, believe me when I say that an attack is very rare. And most people find it just a little bit harder than being on land. Besides, it's just 800 meters. I see you do more than that in your sleep during gym class."

"It isn't the distance," I said, feeling more nervous than ever as Kellen and four of his fellow swimmers walked toward us in nothing but their Speedo briefs. I didn't know where to look suddenly.

It's the salt.

Chapter Twelve

"There's nothing to eat." I stood in front of the mini fridge of the camper, staring into its hollow case. "And I mean that literally."

I'd been at Hailey's when she whined to her mom that they had "nothing to eat," when the shelves were stocked with bread, bananas, cheese, and milk. What she was really saying, I knew, and her mom knew, and maybe Hailey deep inside knew, was that there was nothing easy to eat that Hailey wanted. Chips and guacamole, bagel pizzas, sugar cereal, frozen waffles.

"I'm sorry," Mom said, rummaging in her drawer for a clean pair of socks. "I know we're running low. I will swing by the store just as soon as I can."

My hair had mostly dried from the pool, but I could still smell the chlorine in the air. All it took was one dip in there to remember why I loved the ocean. The salt maybe dried some people out but not me. It was like a conditioner for my whole body.

"Are you excited about the race?" Mom asked.

I shrugged. "I'm still worried about transforming since it's in the ocean."

"We'll have to practice," she said. "But I know you can do it. You'll just have to work on controlling your emotions. No kisses or fights before the match." She laughed.

I smiled too, hugging my bare shoulders as I stared at our empty cupboards. It was exciting, in a way, to be a part of a team. I'd never felt that before. When other kids were playing soccer after school, or baseball or dance, I'd been either at home in the camper reading until Mom came home or at Hailey's when she didn't have ballet practice. But passing off that ring in the water to Kellen, his fingers brushing mine, was a huge thrill. And hearing the cheers of the rest of the team and Miss Kalowski for me as I pounded through the water was even better.

"I had no idea," Kellen said, racing his hands through his hair. "You are so fast. We're gonna dominate!" He slapped hands with the other guys on the team, the girls casting wary glances in my direction.

I hadn't swum far since my first transformation, but it was crazy how much easier it was now. I was good before, but that was human good. This time, even without my tail, my body seemed to know what to do. I wasn't nearly as fast as I was in the sea with my fin, but I was good. Better than good, actually. Miss Kalowski said that I might even be able to swim with the high school team.

"Mom, when am I going to do my first save?" I turned, trying to ignore the hunger pains in my stomach. I hadn't eaten since lunch, and swimming—even without transforming, always made me ravenous. "You've taught me about how to transform, how to hide it, but when do I get to do that?"

She smiled. "I was waiting for you to ask that question."

"So how does it work?" I asked, remembering I had a granola bar in the bottom of my backpack that had been there for weeks. It would be smashed to pieces by now, but it was still food.

She sat at the dinette, a hairbrush in hand. "It works differently for everyone. Because you are guided to the people in need, it's difficult to describe since it is a heightened sensation. Like transforming. How can you explain the pull of your muscles, and the shift in your organs? But I will say that you will know when it happens."

"So how did it work for you?" I asked, licking the silver wrapper of the bar, my stomach still feeling empty.

"I was sixteen when I had my first save," she said, almost dreamily. "By then I'd been transforming for two years. I was living in South Florida with Grammie and Pop, and since Grammie was more experienced, I figured she was getting most of the calls. I'd been in the water with her when she got one. For her, she felt the ocean quiver a little bit, and would swim in the direction she felt the most motion. But for me, it was completely different."

Someone slammed a camper door nearby but she didn't startle at all. Her eyes were fixed on the wall straight ahead.

"I was pushing myself that day. I knew I wasn't fast enough to get out as far as I wanted for certain saves and that bothered me. So I had this old waterproof watch of Pops and was timing myself. I was so tired and about to come in when I felt it." She paused. "It was like the sound of wind and waves were screaming for me, but it was so far away that I couldn't make it out. So I started swimming toward the screaming, and the closer I got, the louder it became, until I got to the shipwreck."

She smiled a little. "It was one of the biggest jobs I've ever done, and it was my first. Some immigrant fishermen, too poor for a lifeboat, too far out for the signals to reach shore. They'd been treading water for a half hour, I'd guess, and were getting so tired. I knew I had to be quiet since there were four of them. So I dove down, looking for their sunken ship. It was getting dark, and I could barely see but I managed to break off a piece of the mast and let it float up to them."

She grinned, "I could almost hear their cries of joy when the mast came up, because they had nothing to hold onto before. Once they all had a hold on it, I got behind it, and I pushed it to shore. It was easy to push, but hard to hide myself. I had to keep readjusting my arms so that my body was covered and I was kicking down instead of out on the surface."

"And they didn't see you?" I asked. "I thought saves were always a drowning person, or someone who needed to return to their ship or something."

"Oh no," Mom said, shaking her head. "No. Saves are all different. And there are different types. Sometimes you are rescuing and reviving a drowning person and carrying them to land. On those you usually have to do our version of mouth-to-mouth to make sure they're breathing if there's no one else around. But sometimes you are repairing cracks in boats with your resin kit. Or pushing the water a certain way so that their lifeboat finds shore. Or warding off sharks from someone completely capable of swimming back themselves."

"Sharks!"

"Yes," she said with a grin. "But you're faster than they are, so it's fine. No one save is the same. But the important thing is to stay hidden. And if there's no way you can do that, then disappear as soon as you know they're safe. Most of the time they think they just imagined the whole thing." She laughed a little. "You'd be surprised at the things humans brush off. Of course, most of them probably ask themselves who would believe them if they did tell anyone. And the answer is no one."

Her face grew darker, her eyebrows furrowing. "It's something I've been thinking a lot about. We've all lost our sense of wonder. Maybe it's science, or the drudge of a commute and daily life, but it's missing in most of us. People don't believe that something strange could exist. It's all easily explained. They don't want to take a chance on something that could be different than what they're used to."

I frowned, sensing that she was talking about more than just the people she saved now.

"Mom, how is the job hunt going?"

She crossed her arms over each other. "I interviewed today to answer phones at an office building. The hours are not what I want, but the pay is okay."

"Did it not go well?" I asked.

She took a deep breath before responding, her hairbrush so full of her long wavy hair that she had to clean it before running it through again. "The man who interviewed me is one I saved."

"What?!"

She nodded. "It was years ago. He was drunk and slipped off a dock. He hit his head so hard he passed out. His buddies were all partying. I swam him to shore and pushed him far enough on the beach that the tide wouldn't reach him before bandaging his head."

"Wow," I murmured. Until now, I'd thought that saves were always in the middle of the ocean, for the truly helpless. But apparently the call came for drunk men on the dock too. "I take it he didn't offer you the job."

She shook her head. "He told me I needed a haircut and some new clothes before he could offer me a job. And he told me I talked too much."

"What a jerk."

"He wasn't a jerk," she said. "He was probably telling me what everyone else that interviewed me won't. I have no education, no skills. I don't know how to dress or talk right."

"You saved his life," I argued. I wished I knew where this man was. I would march up to him and tell him how wrong he was not to hire her. How she saved him and didn't ask for anything in return.

"I did," she agreed. "But the skills of the land and the skills of the sea aren't the same. And that's why I want you to stay in school, Cass." She stood and slipped her flip-flops on. "You need to survive in this world. No one pays you to save lives. It's something you do because you love it."

"Where are you going?" I asked as she reached for the camper door.

"To fish." She turned, giving me a sad smile. "I'm not going to let my baby go hungry."

We went out together that night after a sad meal of catfish and a couple anchovies. The camper would never smell the same again but at least our stomachs were full.

I transformed on my first memory that day, but I didn't tell Mom what it was. It was one of my oldest. Me and her and my dad at a park on a summer day. We had a basket full of bread and strawberries, and they weren't fighting.

Dad chased me around the grass, his beard tickling me once he caught me, making Mom laugh. She always told him he had a beautiful beard. I remembered that.

There weren't many memories of him anymore, so I clung to this one. His dark hair, starting to thin a little on top, his hairy arms, and his blue button shirts were all I knew of him. But that day in the park I could never forget. No matter how many lifetimes I had to try. No matter how far away Mom took us.

"Have you ever been seen, Mom?" I asked as we took a break from swimming and bobbed up and down. Her red T-shirt clung to her back, a long, wet braid snaking down it.

"Never."

"What's the secret?"

She dove in for a minute, and when she came back up, she was closer to shore, her eyes sad as she watched the sunset. Had I ever noticed how sad my mom was before I found out who she really was?

"People aren't looking for you. If they were, they might see you."

We swam in silence after that, but the ocean roared in a way I'd never heard before. A rumble sounded through the water, like a warning. Pulse-pulse-pulsing, telling me to swim faster, to get away. Almost like the air and the wind and the waves were warning me to run.

Chapter Thirteen

The day of the meet I woke with a tangle of nerves, and not because I was afraid we would lose. I knew we would win. Between me and Kellen and this other kid on his team appropriately nicknamed Fish, we were unstoppable. I was worried about shifting. Of my tail peeking up through the water and my mom and I being forced to swim away to another continent where they'd never find us. NBD.

"Just remember to keep your thoughts on the race," Mom reminded me. She picked me up at school, not seeming to notice the stares from kids in all directions. She wore a denim skirt that buttoned in the front. I couldn't remember a time when she did not have that skirt. She paired it with an old T-shirt that had a picture of a giant mushroom on it with the words, "I'm a fungi," beside it. But it was her hair, the almost floor length waves, straggly and brown, with gray pieces beginning to show on top that I knew they were really staring at.

I pulled her arm away from them and walked with her to the city bus stop.

"It's not enough to just keep your emotions from getting out of hand. It helps to have something else to think about. It keeps your thoughts filled, so there's no space for a random emotion to sneak in."

I rested my head on the back of the bus shelter. A woman was smoking nearby, shuffling her feet back and forth and stopping to release a circle of gray smoke. I gave her a little wave when she caught me looking at her. "Was I crazy to agree to do this?"

Mom shook her head. "No. You were brave. And I'm proud of you. Is Hailey coming?"

"Is Hailey coming," I laughed. "Oh Mom."

I could hear her before I saw her. She must have recruited all of the other friends she had besides me to film her. I spotted Laura from her science class, Libby and Britt from ballet, all holding phones or cameras, watching the boy swimmers nearby with longing in their eyes.

"Cass!" she yelled at me as we walked toward her. My stomach was in knots, thinking about transforming in front of Kellen. What if the entire school saw my tail? Or worse, my butt?

When I got to her, she hugged me like I was the only donut left on Earth and I remembered why I loved Hailey so much, even though she drove me crazy. "Man, this thing is nuts! I had no idea it was such a big deal. No wonder Kellen bugged you so much about it." I looked around the crowded beach. I recognized a lot of kids from school and a few teachers too. Principal Lyons was there, along with Kellen's parents.

"I didn't know it was such a big deal either," I said as some girls from another school brushed past me.

All of a sudden, I felt incredibly awkward and big. My arms and legs were so long and weird. Not to mention I didn't even think about shaving them, which now seemed like a huge oversight. I didn't even own a razor.

The wind was picking up, sending low swells of white waves crashing down on the sand. I thought I felt a raindrop.

"Can you do a quick interview with me?" Hailey asked. "Pleeeease? Nothing big, I promise. Just a quick, 'Hey, Haiz subscribers. Are you ready to watch St. Johns dominate Cliffwood and Bleaker?"

"Conditions aren't ideal," Mom said, hanging around next to us and surveying the crowd with a smile.

Some boys from my team walked past with their blue school jackets on. "Hey, Cass, we're going to do some warm-ups in a bit," one of them said. Robbie, I think, with Fish on his left. I saw them both look at Mom, snickering at her goofy face turned to the sky.

I felt myself blush and then shook my head. She was my mom. They had no idea what she was like. But between my awkward body and her embarrassing outfit and hair, I had a hard time getting their laughing out of my head.

"Okay let's do it quick," I told Hailey, letting her lead me to her group of friends.

"So wait, what am I saying?"

"Just like, 'Hey, Haiz subscribers. Ready to watch St. Johns dominate Bleaker and Cliffwood?' And then just, do something crazy! Like, jump on my back or something, or stick your tongue out and lick some sand. I don't know. Something weird."

"Lick sand? What?"

"Hey, Cass!" I turned as Kellen headed right for us. Immediately Laura, Libby, and Britt looked up, giggling as he came closer. I always wondered why girls did that. I always had the opposite reaction. Nothing was funny when a cute guy was around. My brain froze. I couldn't laugh if I tried.

"Hi," I waved. I think I waved.

"You coming to the team meeting?"

"Yeah."

I started to go but Hailey caught me by the arm. "Real quick!"

I turned to her friends and said, "Hey, Haiz people! Stick around to watch St. Johns swim dominate Bleaker and Cliffwood." Then I put my hands in the pocket of my hoodie.

"That'll have to work," Hailey grunted as I ran after Kellen, waving to my mom who was walking towards the water, smiling at the seagulls that circled overhead, people staring at her like she was crazy.

The rest of the team huddled around Miss Kalowski, whose frizzy white-blonde hair blew over her face as she spoke. "'Kay guys, here's the deal. They wanted to postpone the meet because of the weather." She motioned at the waves that were beginning to pick up. "But we said no way. Conditions are still safe enough to swim. But if you feel like you're starting to lose control or you start to panic, just wave your hand up and bob. No one's going to be mad at you."

Robbie grunted next to me, shaking his head 'no' at the other girls on his team, his icy gray eyes landing on mine.

"You're going to paddle out there. Take your time. Once you get to the green lane—that's ours on the far end, hold onto the lifeboats until it's your turn to swim. And whatever you do," she paused, "Don't forget that we're a team. We've worked for this together, and we're going to win this together. You hear me?" She grinned, putting her arm around my shoulder and squeezing. "Now let's swim."

I pulled off my hoodie and pants reluctantly, telling myself not to pick my wedgie no matter how bad it was getting. The water was colder than I expected. There were cheers behind us. People hooting and calling out specific names. The boys were ahead of the girls, and I held back, walking behind them all. Not really a part of the team even if I would be the one to carry them to victory. Why had I not realized that until now? They didn't care about me, not really. They just wanted to win.

When it got too hard to walk, we started to paddle out, the two other schools beside us. "Amazon woman," I heard a girl in gray whisper to her friend over the waves. They both turned around and giggled.

Focus, I told myself. *No emotions. Close it out.*

But I felt something flutter inside of me. And as much as I wanted to block it out, it was impossible to ignore completely. My body ached to transform. It felt almost hungry for it.

I turned around to go back in, feet already sinking in the sand. My team would have to deal with the consequences. They didn't like me anyway.

I waved at Miss Kolawski, whose eyes were wide as she looked at me. She shook her head back and forth mouthing the word, "No. No." Her hands up in the air.

I fought the nerves in my chest as I paddled back. I couldn't do this. I was so, so stupid.

But as I rose up, I felt a hand meet mine, wet and cold, beneath the water. I turned to see Kellen's face. "You can do this, Cass," he said, before spitting out a mouthful of seawater.

"I can't," I murmured, fear trapping me in, like a fish on a dock, wriggling for freedom. He had no idea.

"You can. And I hope you do. But not for me. And not for any of those losers." He jerked his thumb back to where the rest of the team was waiting for me, sitting on their lifeboats, watching me with angry faces.

"Do it for you. Because you're good. And people deserve to know that."

"Ow ow!" I heard Hailey call from the beach. "Go Cassie!"

I caught a glimpse of Mom, her face worried as she stared out—not at me, but at the ocean, a frown crossing her face.

"I don't think I can," I whispered, my face crumpling. Oh my gosh I was crying in front of Kellen. Give me the ice age back. I'd take the ice age any day.

"You're the best swimmer in the water right now," he said seriously. "Way better than me. Way better than Fish."

A huge wave came, pushing me backward as I stared at the teams, all ready to go and waiting for me to get there. I stumbled and then stood, nodding at him, thinking of the people who laughed at me, at my mom. Of all the times someone told me my clothes smelled bad. Who asked why I lived in a camper and took the city bus. I thought of my dad briefly too, but wasn't sure why. Maybe a part of me wished I had him here to watch me in my first ever competition.

"You're right," I said, diving headfirst back into the water, kicking my arms and legs out in controlled strokes that got me to the lifeboats faster than I even anticipated.

A couple moments later Kellen appeared next to me, helping me onto the boat that was beginning to rock from the weight of the waves. "Thanks, Cass," he said, ignoring the stares of his friends and the girls on the team.

A low quiver raced through me again, but I pushed it back. "Let's win," I said in return, as the ocean begin to scream.

And then the whistle blew.

Chapter Fourteen

Mara went first, our slowest swimmer which was Miss Kalowski's plan. She stacked me and Fish and Kellen at the end, hoping that we could make up for whatever lost time there was. Bleaker and Cliffwood's girls were creaming her. But she made it back, tagging Robbie, who jumped from the boat and began swimming with a vengeance.

I scanned the beach for my mom. Where was she? Everyone on shore was shouting, holding signs, jumping up and down as their swimmer got back to the boat. But Mom was nowhere in sight.

Kellen jumped in the water, trying to make up for lost time. We were almost 300 feet behind Bleaker, and Cliffwood was at the front. When he got back it would be my turn to swim. Where was she?

"Cass, you're on deck," Fish said, his teeth already chattering. The wind was picking up, sending cold sprays of ocean water on us. "You got this."

I rubbed my hands together, trying to forget that Mom was gone, that there was a possibility I would transform right here, in front of all of these people. She told me no fights or kisses before the race. But what about nerves?

Kellen tagged me and I took the ring from him, plunging into the ocean, my muscles relaxing as I beat the waves, keeping my feet together like I did with my fins.

Blank thoughts, blank thoughts, I thought to myself. Don't feel anything. You can do it.

But beneath the roar of the voice in my head, I heard something else. A call, like the flap of a bird's wings. Like the beating heart of the ocean floor. Something tugged at me as I reached the other side, turning around to get back to my team.

When I rose into the air to breathe, I heard the cheering of the crowd. They were louder, much louder than before. But when I plunged into the water, it was not still. It was like the ocean was screaming for me. Tugging at me so fiercely that it took everything in me not to let myself go and allow the saltwater to change me.

Mom, I thought as I rose for air, *Mom are you hearing this?*

But then I was at the lifeboat, being pulled up as Fish took the ring from my fingers, the rest of my team clapping my back, someone handing me a blanket, my teeth chattering as I looked down frantically and saw my two hairy, white legs shaking.

"You set a record!" Kellen said, whooping as Fish tore up the water. "We have a huge lead!"

I saw Miss Kalowski clapping on the beach, almost dancing with excitement as Fish turned, Bleaker and Cliffwood's swimmers trailing behind him.

"You won this for us!" Kellen yelled over the waves, brushing wet bits of hair from his face. "You won it!"

When Fish returned, handing the ring to the boat leader, the entire team erupted, as well as half of the people on the beach.

My smile was so wide I couldn't think straight. We rowed onto shore, the team spilling out into the water once it got shallow, racing through the sand.

Miss Kalowski picked me up and spun me around, her face so excited. "You set a record!" she yelled over the roar of other parents and students. "You're unbelievable!" She gathered the team in a huddle and we all put our hands in, yelling, "St. Johns!"

Hailey fought her way through the crowd with her friends. "You're a freaking fish!" she yelled jumping on my back. "You're not human!" A ripple of shock raced through me until I realized she didn't mean that literally.

"Best friend right here!" she yelled.

74

My heart was so full that I didn't wonder where Mom was until people began to clean up the beach, kids going home with their parents in vans and SUVs.

Mrs. Pederson waved at me from across the beach. "Do you want a ride home, Cass?"

I shook my head. "I'll take the bus! I'm just waiting for my mom."

She smiled sadly and waved goodbye as I trudged along the sand, getting closer to the ocean.

"Mom?" I said out loud. There were just a few stragglers left, but no one was in the water. "Mom?"

I stepped into the water and felt it again, a low throbbing beneath the water, more of a sensation than a sound. So loud without the noise of the crowd on the beach that I couldn't ignore it any longer. I threw my sweatshirt and pants on the beach and dove in.

With my ears beneath the water, it sounded less like a pulsing heart and more like a scream. So loud it pained me. I hated it. I wanted it to stop.

Once I was far enough out, I let myself transform. It was more of a decision this time and less controlled by my emotions. The pain was almost nothing now. My muscles knew what to do. In fact, it felt like a relief in a way to be in the water and not fight it anymore.

Mom, I thought again, beneath the water, trying to find her even with the pounding heartbeat of the ocean. *Mom.*

The current tugged at me, pulling me deeper into the water and I obeyed, feeling more urgent now than I had just moments ago with a crowd of people watching me and Kellen waiting on the lifeboat. I thrashed through the waves, my muscles so fueled with energy that I couldn't contain it. Faster and faster I pumped, my arms and fin bringing me closer to the center of the beating, the ocean's roar so loud that I could no longer hear the sound of my own breathing.

And then I saw Mom's fin. Just for a moment, before I saw the body in her hands. I shimmied through the surface to meet her. Never in my life did I want something so much.

"Cass," Mom said, breathless as she watched me appear beside her. She had a man in one of her arms, his head lolled to the side. And in her other arm was a child, no older than two, whose whimpering wails softened when she saw me appear.

"Refugees," Mom said. "I'm not sure where they're coming from. But a wave capsized their boat. I already took the two others to shore. A woman and another child."

"You left the baby with an unconscious guy?"

She shook her head. "He was conscious. In the best shape. I induced this."

My mouth gaped. "I'll explain it later. Will you take the child?" Mom asked. "Her mother will be missing her."

I reached for the child, whose tears continued. I pulled her close to me, both arms wrapping around her middle and kicked through the waves, surprised at the thrill that swept through me then. I knew it would be amazing. My first save. But I had no idea it would happen this quickly.

"She's sweet, isn't she? I remember when you were that small," Mom said as we swam the two to safety. They were much farther out than I realized at first. If it weren't for us, they wouldn't have made it to shore at all. It would have taken days to get there. How fast was I, really? How deep in the ocean did my body take me?

"She is," I said as the child watched me with wide eyes before bursting into tears again. "Shh. Shh," I said, rubbing her back with my wet hand. "You're safe now. You're all safe."

"You're good at this," Mom said to me as she swam with the man almost twice her size effortlessly through the rolling waves.

"At swimming?" I asked.

"At saving."

We were quiet the rest of our swim as it began to rain. Drops showered down, the wind picking up even more. I held the baby close to me, singing to her as I swam, keeping her face from getting hit by the waves. "Shh," I comforted her.

Soon I realized that the ocean was no longer roaring. That even though the wind and waves and rain were picking up, it was still. That must be the feeling that came when a mission was complete. When we reached the people in distress in time.

All at once I caught sight of the red and blue flashes, emergency vehicles on the beach ahead. "What do we do, Mom?" I asked frantically. "They'll see us!"

She grinned. "This is a good thing. We did our part in the water, and the professionals are taking over the land now."

"But the guy."

He was still draped across Mom's back, his head bobbing against her shoulder. We were close enough to the sand now that I could see another woman with an older child—maybe three years old, sitting on the beach and watching the waves. "I'll take care of him," she said. "What I need you to do is lay the baby on her back."

"No way!" I said, pulling her to me.

"Yes," she said gently. "She'll float. And then I need you to swim back so you are hidden. Can you do that for me?"

I pressed the child closer. She was no longer crying, but clung to me, not wanting to let me go. "You're safe now," I whispered, releasing her into the waves.

She screamed out but kept her head above water.

"Go, Cass!"

I bobbed underwater but turned in time to see Mom take a deep breath, and in front of me, and his daughter, covered his mouth with her own. She did it three times, before the man began to shake, rising up for air like he'd been drowning, and flapping his arms in a panic.

When he saw his daughter, floating just a few feet from him, he began to swim, saying over and over, "Maria! Maria!"

Mom appeared beside me, pulling my shoulder until we were touching, both of us bobbing in the ocean, watching the scene on land unfold.

The emergency personnel sent a boat out into the water, paddling the man and little Maria to shore. I watched as his wife broke down, yelling for her husband, the child beside her clapping her hands.

"Is it always this amazing?" I asked, tears pricking my eyes at the sight. If I thought winning that race was amazing, this was ten times better. A thousand times better.

"No," Mom said. "Sometimes you end up covered in floating vomit and pull some drunk guys out of dirty dock water." She grinned lazily. "But sometimes you get this."

We began our swim back, the ocean so quiet now that all I could hear was the waves, the wind, my own heartbeat pounding in my ears.

"Did you win?" she asked when we were back at home in the camper. Mom had some soup she got from volunteering at the food bank that week and canned chicken noodle had never tasted so good.

"We did."

"I knew you would! I'm so sorry I missed it. I got the call and I fought it as long as I could. But I figured you would understand."

I thought of all the times my mom ran out on me at the diner, or missed parent-teacher conferences or came home late. I was so angry at her, so confused at where she was going and why she was always missing. "I understand now," I said. I could still feel the arms of that little girl in the water, wrapped tight around me. "I'm glad you missed it."

She grinned. "I think you're probably the only kid in the world to ever say that to their parents."

I nodded over a spoonful of soup. "Probably true."

Chapter Fifteen

"**C**ASSSSSS!"

Half the lunchroom turned to stare as I entered and I suddenly felt embarrassed about my too-short T-shirt and torn jeans. Hailey almost jumped on me, wrapping me up in the biggest hug ever. "I got over 4,000 views on my YouTube channel! All thanks to you!"

"Huh?" I asked, letting her lead me away from the line to sit at a table. She pulled out her phone. "Check it out. Oh my gosh we're up to 4,200! What the—? Thank you, Cass! Oh my gosh. Oh my gosh!"

I pulled the phone from her, pressing play on the center of the red screen. A pop up of Hailey came up at the beach. "Hey guys! I'm Haiz! Welcome to my channel. Please subscribe in the box below or I'm gonna be sad." She made a pouty puppy dog face before jumping in the sand. "I'm here today to film my best friend forever Cass, who joined the swim team like, two days ago so she could do this meet and oh my gosh, she is freaking fast. Just wait and see."

Then there was about two minutes of Hailey doing selfies and silly faces with Libby, Britt and Laura before the race started. I gripped the screen tighter as the first swimmer started, watching Mara's slow crawl to the end of the lane.

"And then I cut because it was super boring," Hailey said, breathing over my shoulder. "But I filmed enough of it for them to be able to see you save the day at the end." I looked back down at the screen as Kellen dove from his boat when something shiny caught my eye just beyond him.

My heart sank. "You're on deck," Hailey said nervously, like she hadn't watched it already a million times. "Okay . . . Ready, steady."

"Hold on," I said, "I just need to scroll back a tiny bit."

I scrolled back until right before Kellen jumped and Hailey snickered. "Can't blame you for wanting to see him jump in the water. I've watched that part like a hundred times. Those abs really glow, don't they?"

I ignored her, focusing on the light in the background. An announcer said, "Kellen Levinson on deck now. One of the strongest swimmers at St. John's, he—" Just then I caught it—a glimpse of a fin in the background, shiny and green, the light just catching it before it disappeared. I felt sweat pool along my hairline. Mom. How could she have let that happen?

"Now you!" Hailey screamed.

By now a few other kids were standing around us, peering over the screen. My body charged through the ocean. I had no idea that I easily passed one Bleaker and two Cliffwood kids in the time I raced. The crowd erupted around Hailey, and the camera bounced up and down as I assumed someone holding it was jumping as well.

"That's your friend?" I heard Britt say over the music Hailey set the race to. Her words were tinged with jealousy. "I like, didn't even know she went to St. John's." There was giggling in the background. I tried to ignore the bitterness in her voice.

"I mean—it's unreal. I put all this time into developing my other videos and this one just takes off. I actually had a news station contact me last night about using it for a story! It ran on a couple networks! Can you believe it? And the comments are just unreal."

I eyed the lunchroom lines that were beginning to die down. They'd stop serving soon and I couldn't afford to miss my main meal of the day. "I gotta eat," I told her.

"'Kay, I'll come with." She linked her arm through mine. "So one troll said all this crap about how you're a girl and shouldn't be able to swim faster than the boys, but don't worry, the feminist commenters shut him down. And then there were some comments about how Bleaker got robbed, but you know that was just some kids on the team that were mad about it. And then there were some about a giant fish in the background. Supposedly there's a big one in the water right when Kellen is about to jump but I haven't been able to see anything. I watched that part like a hundred times—"

"A big fish?" I asked, accepting the lunch tray that was, appropriately, fish sticks and soggy crinkle fries. I grabbed an apple and a banana from the bowl at the end, as well as the extra containers of broccoli and coleslaw.

Hailey wrinkled her nose. "Yeah, a big fish. A green one or something. Someone said it looked like a mermaid! Can you believe that? Haha. Maybe that's why the video did so well . . ."

I had to sit down. Somewhere. Anywhere. I plopped at the end of a table full of popular girls, all of them scooting down so they wouldn't have to talk to me. They huddled close together to continue their conversation.

Hailey perched beside me. "Anyway, I'm just so lucky you're my friend. You're the bestest. I can't wait for your next meet. When is it? Maybe you could do a follow-up interview with me? After school or something?"

"Sure, Haiz," I said, scarfing the food down as fast as I could, ignoring the stares of the popular girls who made faces from across the table.

"Hey, Cass," Kellen said from out of nowhere, waving a couple feet away with some other guys from the team.

I looked up, half a fish stick in my mouth and waved with a couple fingers.

"*Hey* Kellen!" one of the popular girls said. Olivia Reynolds.

"Oh hey," he said, waving as he walked away.

"Did you see that?" Hailey whispered loud enough for the other girls to hear. "You've made it."

"Come on, Haiz," I said. But inside I felt my insides flutter so fast I had to take a deep breath to calm them.

"Can you come over today?" she asked. "After school? We can film it then."

I shook my head. "Not today. I have to do something with my mom." *I have to tell my Mom something*, I thought. *Tell her that her fin was caught on camera*. My excitement about Kellen and the race quickly faded.

Hailey's pouty face came back. "I thought that—"

Her phone began to ring as we got the final bell to go to class.

"Who is it?" I asked, afraid for a minute it was a news station, about to do a big story on the mermaid fin caught on camera.

"The Waffle Stop," she said, handing it to me. "I'm guessing it's for you."

I ran off the bus after school, hoping Mom wouldn't worry too much about me. Shara called Hailey's phone saying that Megan and Lorna both quit and she'd been waiting tables all morning and would I please get there as soon as school got out and she would pay me hourly and let me keep tips.

After eating soup from the food bank every night lately, the hourly and tips would be huge for me and Mom. One shift, if I worked hard enough, might be enough to pay our camper rent.

"You're here," Shara said as I stepped in the door, standing back against the counter to catch her breath.

She was wearing a yellow waitress uniform, the buttons so tight across her chest that I seriously hoped the customers were wearing protective eyewear. "You would not believe this day. Two servers quit in one day! Just up and left."

"Why?" I asked, reaching for a dress from the shelf and pulling it over my school clothes.

"Something about being overworked. I don't know." She leaned back against the counter, rubbing her eyes beneath her glasses.

I raised my eyebrows and she frowned at me. "Thank God your little ballerina friend answered the phone. You know, we really need to get you a cell phone."

I perked up a little at that idea. If she needed me bad enough maybe she'd buy me one. "No worries. I'm here now and can stay as late as you need."

Luis waved from the kitchen tiredly. He stood at the stove, frying a couple eggs, the stink of sausage and bacon circling him. "Yo Cass!"

"I've got tables eight and four that need their checks. Two needs water and coffee refills. One needs his order taken. He's been waiting awhile. Can you handle it?"

"Yup. Got it."

She waved at the door. "Get going then. I've got to see if I can hire some new girls before tomorrow."

"My mom is still free," I offered bravely.

But she just shook her head, waddling back into her office.

I ran out the kitchen door, a pitcher of water and coffee in each hand. I stopped at table two, an angry looking couple shooting darts at me from their eyes. "We've been waiting for fifteen minutes. He has to get back to work!"

"So sorry," I replied. "We're short-staffed today." I kept my eyes on the table. "Anything else I can get you?"

"The check!" When I was only two feet away, I could hear her lean closer to her boyfriend and say, "She looks like she's like, twelve. So don't worry about a tip. Probably the owner's kid or something."

I grimaced, moving on to table one, my face burning from her comment. "So sorry, sir, I'll be right with you. Let me just get these checks out so the other folks can leave."

"Take your time," the voice responded.

Frantically, I raced into the kitchen, printing off the three checks and delivered them, as all three tables stood immediately, clearing the restaurant except for table one.

My shoulders sagged as I walked toward it. "So sorry, sir, we've had a big rush and we're short staffed." I laughed a little. "Sorry, did I already say that? What would you like?"

I looked up from my pad of paper at the face in front of me, stepping back at the familiarity. He had a receding hairline, strands of hair brushed back behind his ears. He wore a gray suit but no tie, and his eyes—his eyes were smiling at me.

I dropped the pad, reaching over to pick it up so he wouldn't see the burning in my face even though I was sure he could hear my heart pounding—louder than it ever had, so loud it could bounce right out of my body.

"Hello, Cass," he said, a smile spreading across his face. "It's so wonderful to see you again."

Chapter Sixteen

"**D**o I know you?" I asked him. But I did know him. Or Ari, at least, had.

She knew him by the click of the lock at the door every night at 5:30. The barrel of his chest as he picked her up and held her upside down, asking her Mom if she'd seen his monkey lately. She knew him by his nighttime stories, deep yawns, and good night kisses. She knew him by his presence once, and then his absence and the stories she made up about him. She knew his ghost.

He smiled sadly. "I wish you did."

"I have to go. We're short staffed today. It's—"

"There's no one else here," he said, gesturing to the empty restaurant. He was right. In the hours after school and before the dinner rush, we were usually slow, with the occasional high school student or elderly couple coming in for an early dinner.

"How did—" I began, brushing a loose piece of hair from my face. "How did you find us? How—"

"I saw you on the news," he said, his face brightening. "They showed a clip last night about the amazing swimmer who has had no formal training. And I got on the next flight. As for finding you here, well, it was a bit of a lucky guess. But your mom always had a soft spot for waffles."

I shifted a little, not sure why I felt uncomfortable about his story. But was it just because he was my dad and my mom had made him this big mystery my entire life? And if he saw me on the news, had he also seen the clip of Mom?

"I, uh—"

"Cass!" Shara waved from the kitchen, her fake smiling angry face on. "We have a new customer!"

"Right. I uh—I gotta go," I said motioning to the two old ladies at the door.

"I understand. I'll just wait here until you get off your shift. We have a lot of catching up to do."

"Actually," I began, "It's not until pretty late. But I could meet you after?"

"I'd like that very much. What time is your shift done?"

I frowned. Since Shara was so short-staffed she probably wanted me to stay until at least ten o'clock when her night shift came in. But if I told her I had homework she'd probably be okay with me leaving around nine. "I'm off at nine," I said quickly.

He was already standing, putting on his coat. "I'll be here for you at nine then." He reached out for a hug, but I stepped back awkwardly.

"I'm gonna just—" I pointed at the couple.

"Of course."

I can't remember what I said to the couple, or which table I sat them at. But later Shara yelled at me for putting them on eight instead of six, which wasn't even cleared yet. I guess one of the women complained to her about getting a smear of maple syrup across her butt.

All I remember was clearing table one where my dad sat. My Dad. And finding a $100 bill and a note beneath his coffee mug.

I'm sorry I showed up here without warning you. I understand if you're not ready to speak to me tonight. But when you are, call me at this number. 894-343-2224. I'm staying in town and would consider it a great honor to get to know you.

—Ken

"You're home!" Mom said as I came in. It was eleven o'clock. The soonest I could get Shara to let me go.

I couldn't remember a time when I felt stranger than I did today. One minute I was so happy I could explode—my hand reaching for that note from him, the $100 bill in my pocket, and the next I was angry. So angry that it took him so long. Angry that Mom dragged us away all those years before without a word. Angry at the universe who decided it was okay for a girl who was also half fish to have such messed up parents.

"Yeah." I let her hug me, lacing her hands through my hair. She smelled like salt and smoke. No doubt from the fish she fried on the stove in the camper. Maybe I'd spend the $100 on some new coals so we could cook our fish outside on the campground grill from now on.

"Hailey's mom called Hobs to tell me where you were," she said. "Really nice of her to do that. How are you? I bet you're beat."

I handed her a take-out box of fried chicken and waffles. I was too nervous after seeing him to eat anything. And besides, there was no time for a break.

"I am."

I fingered the note in my pocket. *I saw Dad,* I could hear myself saying. *He showed up at the Waff Stop. He looked like a million memories and sunny mornings and starry nights.* But I couldn't say it out loud. Mom had her secrets. Why shouldn't I have my own?

"Mom, your fin got caught on Hailey's camera."

Her head snapped up. "What are you talking about?"

"Hailey filmed the meet. And I can see your fin in one of the shots. You must have been going out for the refugee family."

She frowned. "Are you sure, baby? I'm always so careful."

"I promise," I said, sensing the iciness in my voice. Was it because she left my dad without a word to him or any explanation to me? Or was it because I'd been on my feet all night working while she sat here in the camper? "You have to be more careful."

"I'll do that. Honey, what's wrong?" She reached for my head, wanting to cup my chin in her hands but I shook her off, stepping back toward the wall.

"Nothing."

"Was Shara hard on you?" Her voice was defensive. I knew that voice.

"No, she was fine."

"Okay." She studied me. I stared at her frumpy body—her too-small T-shirt without a bra, her cut-off capri pants that were torn on one side. The ratty mane of hair she held back with a sweaty scarf around her head.

"Well, why don't you eat something before you go to bed?"

"I'm not hungry."

"Can I do anything for you before you go to bed?"

"I'm not going to bed, Mom," I said, my voice rising. "I have homework. Because I'm thirteen years old and I just got off work so that we can afford to eat."

"I'm sorry," she said softly. "I'm still looking hard for something. But I sure appreciate what you're doing for us."

I sat at the dinette, pulling my math book out from my backpack. "Sure."

"I'll call the school tomorrow with Hobs phone and excuse you so you can sleep a little. I know you're gonna need to rest—"

"I have a morning shift at the Waff," I cut in, raising my pencil to look at her. "So no. I'll be up in about," I checked the digital clock on the stove, "Six hours."

"Surely Shara can—"

"Please *leave me alone*," I hissed, as a swarm of numbers danced before my eyes. I was so tired. So confused about seeing my dad. So angry at Mom for keeping me from him all of these years. Whatever her reasons were, he was my dad. He loved me once. I knew that.

She walked into the room with her hands up. "Okay. I'm sorry, honey. I'll leave you to your schoolwork."

I woke up hours later to a blaring alarm clock, a pencil smudge on my face and math homework that was wet from drool.

When I left in the morning, Mom was nowhere to be found. But I thought, from the window of the bus, I saw her tail flicker in the morning light.

"Are we okay?" Hailey asked me at lunch. Libby and Britt were saving a seat for her, whispering back and forth as they looked from her to me to each other. I knew they were staring at my clothes. The black pants that were two sizes too big, cinched at the waist with a scarf of Mom's and a too-small pink T-shirt.

"Yeah," I said, getting in line for school lunch. "Why?" I rubbed my eyes sleepily.

"You haven't been over for like, two weeks. You used to come every day."

"I've had a lot going on," I said.

"Like what?" She stuck her hip out, holding a finger up to Libby who was waving her over.

"Stuff with my mom. Work. I don't know."

I ached to tell her about my dad. His note was burning a hole in my pocket, already wrinkled from the number of times I'd pulled it out to read it today, just to make sure that it was real.

"Did I do something to make you mad?"

I shook my head.

"Are you sure?"

I rolled my eyes, looking at Libby and Britt growing more and more impatient. "I think your *friends* over there are trying to talk to you."

She whipped around, crossing her arms as she came back to face me. "You know, they could be your friends too if you would just try a little harder."

"Try harder how?" I was at the front of the line now, nodding a thank you to the lunch ladies who served up some kind of meat patty with refried beans and a cup of strawberry Jell-O.

"Did they like, decide to do leftover day today?" Hailey asked with a wrinkled nose. "It smells so bad. I can't believe you eat that crap."

I turned to her, "I'm sorry I'm poor, Hailey."

"It's not that," she protested. "I don't care if you're poor. You just act poor. You're sad and mopey all the time because you don't have a phone and you have to take the bus. And can't you at least try to get to know my ballet friends? They think you're a snob because you never talk to them."

"They hate me!" I said, louder than I meant to.

A few kids around us turned to stare. "They'll never be my friends," I said a little softer but not much. "Because I'm weird. I have bad clothes and no cell phone and I live in a camper and my mom is a freak. They only know who I am because of you. And if my clothes and my lunch and my camper bug you so much, I don't need you! Go sit with your pretty friends at your pretty table where you all have clothes from the Gap and talk about how many followers you have!"

I didn't realize tears were streaming down my face until now, and I was so angry I threw my entire lunch—tray and all into the nearest trash can.

"No problem! I don't need you either!" she called as I ran out the door. "Go be boring and sad by yourself!"

I ran to the girl's bathroom, ignoring the eighth-grade girls who turned to stare at me and rushed into a stall to mop up my face.

Then I stood up, smoothed my hair back, and made the walk to the front office. I ignored the stares as I passed. I knew my face was blotchy from crying, but I had to do this.

Ms. Oliver greeted me as I walked in the main office. "Hello, Cass! Oh honey, what's wrong?" she asked, brushing back her bright blonde hair. "Have you been crying?"

I nodded. No point trying to hide it. "I need to make a phone call."

"Sure thing, honey. I know how hard middle school can be. Just go right ahead." She passed the phone toward me and I reached in my pocket, feeling around for the crumpled paper even though I didn't need it. I had the number memorized.

"Hey," I said, my voice shaking as I spoke into the receiver. "This is Cass."

Chapter Seventeen

He picked me up from school in his rental car. Black and sleek, nicer than anything I'd ridden in before. I hoped that the other kids saw it as they stepped onto the bus. Hailey, specifically.

"Cass!" my dad said as I climbed in the car. "I'm so happy you called."

He wore a bright blue polo shirt and jeans. I could see that he wasn't fat like a lot of dads I knew. Dark hair grew on his arms—thick like I remembered, even though he was losing it on his head.

"What do you want to do?"

I felt my stomach rumble inside of me, the cafeteria lunch I threw away taunting me. "I'm pretty hungry."

"Let's take care of that! What sounds good?"

"There's a place called Pickles up here," I said a little shyly.

It was pretty expensive. Hailey's parents took us there once. The sandwiches cost almost $9.00 but I thought about it all the time. The warm turkey on a hot bun, served with creamy macaroni and cheese and a sour pickle on the side.

"Sounds great!"

I sat back, unable to fight the rush of happiness at being in a car, with my Dad, going out to eat and knowing he could actually pay for it.

We ordered our food and sat in a booth, waiting for them to bring it to us. "So tell me about school," he said, a little shyly. "Do you get good grades? What are you learning about?"

I started out a little slow. Giving him small bits and pieces of my life. We were reading *And Then There Were None* in English, I got a 98% on my last math test. But then I began to open up, sharing about my swim meet and how good it felt to be good at something. How I managed to work at the Waffle Stop and still do my homework. I spoke about Hailey like we'd never been in a fight, wanting him to know that I had friends. Selling him on my life without really telling the truth.

I'm a superhero, I wanted to say. *Kind of like a mermaid but not. We live in a camper and we have no money but Mom is amazing. She has saved so many lives but she needs a job. Hailey has all of these new friends and she's embarrassed of me. I can't even talk to Kellen, even though I think he might like me too. I'm the only kid in the school without a cell phone.*

"What about you?" I asked, as the food came out. I sunk my teeth into the warm sandwich, which tasted better than anything ever had before. Juicy and crusty and a little spicy. "What do you do?"

He grinned, sitting back to watch me eat. "I teach biology at KWU. In the evenings I train for triathlons. I've done three this year."

I smiled. That explained why he wasn't fat like some of the other dads.

"What are you the best at?" I asked, glad I knew what a triathlon was. "Running, swimming, or biking?"

"Swimming," he said with a smile. "It seems like we have that in common."

He waved the server over at the end of the meal. "Can I get another of that meal to go for her?" he asked kindly. "And add a few chocolate chip cookies to the bag as well."

I couldn't stop smiling as he carried the bag out to the car, whistling as he opened the door for me.

"Where to?" he asked.

I grimaced, thinking about him taking me to the camper where Mom was. I wasn't ready to tell her that he was here. She would freak out, and this afternoon was the best thing that had happened to me in a long time.

"The Waffle Stop," I said, my shoulders sagging a little. "I have a shift tonight."

He looked at me briefly before starting the car. "You know, I would rather have you focus on your studies and your friends than work in the afternoons. Are you and your mother doing all right?"

I cringed when he mentioned Mom's name. It was the first time he'd asked about her at all, I realized. "We're fine," I lied, sinking back against the cool leather of the seat. "I like working."

We drove the rest of the way in silence but before he let me out, he said, "Thank you for spending time with me today, Cass. I really enjoyed getting to know you."

"Thank you for lunch," I said. And then, without thinking, I leaned over the car to give him a hug. He patted my back a couple times before I let go and ran inside the building. I wasn't actually scheduled to work but I knew Shara would be happy to see me.

"Hey Cass," Luis said as I stepped in the back. He was reading a magazine while a tray of frozen waffles rotated on the warming rack. "You look like you just won the lottery. Why so happy?"

I shrugged, pulling on an apron and starting to work on the stacks of dirty dishes piling up on the side of the sink. "Just happy, Luis. Don't know why."

My next couple weeks blended, every day like the one before. My early shift at the Waffle Stop then off to school where I took my lunch into the library and did homework so I wouldn't have to face Hailey. A couple days after school I had swim practice or went into work, but most days I spent with my dad.

He took me to the movies, insisting that I get popcorn and a drink, a smile across his face through the entire thing. We took long walks along the pier, and he told me about my cousin Danny, who was a senior now and the star of the basketball team. I tried not to feel jealous when my dad said that he practiced with Danny a lot growing up, and that he was an assistant coach for his team. He told me about Aunt Margo, who was a nurse at the hospital, and got a little choked up when he said that Grandma was gone now.

We ate a lot. He took me to get spaghetti and meatballs at Sauce, pizza at Mushroom City, tacos at the Sand Shack.

One day he said, "I think we should go shopping." We stood in the mall, the too-bright lights shining down, and I thought about how lucky I was to be there. The luckiest girl in the whole world. We went into stores I'd never even been to and he waited outside the dressing room while I tried things on.

I got some leggings, a pair of high-tops, and a furry vest like the one Hailey had. He bought me some new lip-gloss and asked the lady at the makeup counter to teach me how to put on mascara and blush.

I wasn't sure how to hide all of the presents from Mom, but then figured I'd just tell her I went to the mall with all of the money I made working at the Waffle Stop. Why should all the money I made be hers?

"Thanks, Dad," I said to him when he dropped me off at the Waffle Stop after the mall. I still had never let him see where we lived. I'd never called him Dad before.

"My pleasure," he said with an enormous grin. "Hey wait," he said, before I gathered my bags to leave. "There's something I wanted to talk to you about."

"Yeah?" I thought that maybe he'd want to take me to Orlando to Disney World. Or maybe to the aquarium.

"How would you feel about coming to live in Salina again?"

I thought my heart would fall out of my chest it dropped so hard. I gripped the side of the car. "Like, for the summer?"

"Like, forever," he said with a grin. "Your old room is still waiting for you. We could get you on a competitive swim team so you could possibly train to swim in college. Maybe even the Olympics!" My heart started racing. "You wouldn't have to work here anymore. You could have a normal life, in a normal house like a normal kid. I could get you a cell phone. Help you with your homework. There's lots to do in Kansas. More than you think."

"Really?" I asked, thinking about leaving Hailey and her friends behind. All of the people who made fun of me and thought I was boring and poor. The greasy camper. The trips to the laundromat to wash our clothes. Shara's grumpy face with the buttons that threatened to pop off any minute.

"Really!" he said. "Nothing would make me happier."

"But . . . What about Mom?"

We had never spoken about her before, not really. He didn't ask about what she did or if she knew he was here. I kind of assumed he knew she didn't know.

"Your mother . . ." He shook his head. "Your mom will be okay. You know better than I do that she lives her own life. That she has different priorities." He closed his eyes for a minute. "I hate to think about all of the times you were alone while she . . . she ran out."

He was talking about her transformations. How much did he know about that?

"She's doing important stuff," I said, thinking about the refugee family she left my meet to save. All of a sudden I realized that I hadn't had a save since then.

"Sometimes," he nodded. "But other times . . . I think it's just her way to escape reality when things get too hard."

"Can I think about it?" I asked. I had to get to the bus stop soon or I'd have to wait awhile for the next one in the dark.

"Of course."

"Okay."

I opened the door to go. "Thanks again for everything."

"I'll see you tomorrow?" he asked.

"Yeah."

"Pickles again?"

I grinned. We'd been going there a lot. "Sounds good."

"Hey Cassie?"

"Yeah?"

"I love you."

My hands shook as I carried the bags, loaded with more presents than I had ever had in my entire life, all purchased in one afternoon.

"I love you too," I said.

Chapter Eighteen

Mom was waiting for me at the camper that night, her arms folded across her chest. "Hey Cass," she said, eyeing the shopping bags I was struggling to carry. "What are all of those?"

I shrugged. "Just some stuff. I went to the mall with Hailey after school," I added, doing my best not to stutter.

She nodded, a little sadly, and I wondered if she did it because she knew it was a lie. I'd never really lied to her before, and it felt strange. I'd never had a reason to do it before.

"I was waiting up to see if you wanted to swim, but it's pretty late now. I had another save today. I was wondering if you would get it too but I guess not."

I set my bags on the ground. I didn't know how to tell her sorry for lying without telling her about Dad. And if I told her about Dad, I would have to explain all of it. How he spent time with me, and took me shopping, and asked me if I would come and live with him again in Salina. That part would break her heart.

"Yeah, I have school tomorrow so I better not."

"Have you been at the Waffle Stop a lot?" Mom asked.

I blinked in the light above the camper kitchen, the bulb flickering a bit. Did she know about Dad?

"Yeah, Shara has had me come in a lot this week."

"Is everything okay with Hailey?"

I shrugged. "Why do you ask?"

"Because I love you."

"It's fine."

"What about school?"

"Also fine."

I yawned, stretching my arms up, already excited about what I would wear to school tomorrow. What Hailey would think when she saw me in the halls. What Kellen would think . . .

"Well will you pencil me in tomorrow?" she asked. "I'd really like to swim with you. There's a lot we haven't talked about. How to get your medical pack together, how to ward off predators. I haven't shown you how to give temporary gills to a human."

"You can do that?" I asked, suddenly intrigued.

She nodded. "Yes. There's so much to go over. I don't expect you to learn it all at once, but we need to get started on it."

Even talking about the water did something to me. I felt my skin begin to itch, like it had been too long since I'd been in and it was calling to me now. Why couldn't Dad have shown up a couple years ago? Or in a couple years from now when I had the whole mermaid thing figured out? The timing was off.

"I have plans tomorrow," I said reluctantly. Dad was taking me to Pickles again. "Work. Shara wants me to come in." It pained me to lie to her, but it had to be done. She could never know Dad was here.

Mom frowned. "Well, maybe when you get off."

"It will be late," I said quickly.

She licked her lips. "Okay. Well maybe this weekend."

"Maybe."

"Are you still excited about this?" she asked, concern dotting her face. "I remember after my transformation you couldn't keep me out of the water. I wanted to do it all, figure all of it out. But it seems like you're not as interested now."

I put my bags under the bunk and slipped off my shoes. I was annoyed with her for asking so many questions when I just wanted to go to bed. *Dad would never ask me all of these questions,* I thought. He would let me do my own thing. "That's because unlike you when you transformed, I actually have a life," I said. "Friends and a job, and I get all A's in school because I try." The words tasted sharp leaving my tongue. "Besides, Mom, somebody has to pay for our food and house. And it sure isn't you. Why don't you go back to school or get a real job? Why don't you grow up and take care of me? Why can't you stop saving other people and save our family?" My words pierced the air, surprising even me.

She froze, her body still, but her eyes were watching mine. "I'm sorry," she said softly, her lips pursed. "Thank you for everything you're doing for us."

I felt my heart sink. I shouldn't have said that. "Mom, I—"

"It's okay," she said quickly. "You're right."

She stepped to the camper door. "Well, I'm going to take a dip, but you get some sleep, okay? I love you," she said before closing the door behind her.

I rolled my eyes, but I hated myself for doing it. For lying to her. For being embarrassed of her. For wishing, that for once, I was a normal girl in Salina, Kansas who wasn't half-fish.

Hailey eyed me in the hallway as I passed her. She wanted me to be the first one to look away and she won. *She always won*, I thought. Our entire friendship she'd been the one who decided what and when and how we should do things. Maybe that's why she liked being my friend. Because she felt big next to my smallness. Because I said yes to her all the time. Because I made her feel good about herself with my awkwardness and bad clothes and school lunch.

I felt like a phony in the fur vest and high-tops, that I put on after work this morning so Mom wouldn't see them. Last night I thought they would transform me into a new person, that people liked—that I liked. But they just made me feel sad.

On my way to the library at lunch, Kellen and his friends passed me. Before I reached the door, he was behind me, his hands gripping his backpack straps. "Hey, Cass."

"Hi," I said, turning to meet him. Wow he was so hot. His cheeks were tanned, his navy-blue shirt pulling out the color in his eyes. Even the peeling skin on his lips was cute somehow.

"Hey so, uh, you haven't been to practice in awhile. Since the meet. Are you coming today?"

My shoulders sagged. Of course that was why he wanted to talk to me. "I uh," I started, feeling my head began to freeze up again. "I have plans today."

"It'd be kind of lame to ditch out on the team again," he said, his eyes narrowing. "We have state coming up."

I looked up. Hadn't he told me that they only needed me for that one meet? "Yeah," I said, my tongue frozen up in the back of my mind, so much anger and frustration pooling in me I couldn't breathe.

"So you'll be there?" he pressed.

"Yeah," I said, wanting more than anything to be anonymous in a booth in the library. To be left alone with my math homework.

"'Kay, cool," he said, already halfway down the hall, fist bumping his friends before pulling his phone out of his pocket.

I sat down inside the library and pulled my sweatshirt over my head, shutting out the noise, the people, the light from getting any deeper into my mind.

Dad picked me up from school in the black car again. "Hey kiddo," he said. "Looking good in your new clothes!"

I stood at the door of the car. "I forgot I had swim practice today."

"Great!" he said. "I'll come watch."

I stepped back in surprise. "Really? It's super boring."

He shook his head. "Cass, I've been waiting my whole life to watch you swim in person. I'll love every minute of it."

I swam harder in practice than I ever had before. Kellen and Fish and the other guys even stopped in their lanes to watch as I tore down, the other girls on my team clapping when I finished.

"She's not real," I heard a guy say to Kellen. "Like, that's not even real."

Ms. Kolawski pulled Dad aside after practice. I couldn't hear everything she said, but I picked up something about school record, the right training, Olympics.

His smile was so big when we got into the car afterward it looked almost painful. I tried to smile back, but the same sad knot in my stomach from last night and earlier today wouldn't leave.

He glanced at me. "Is everything okay?"

"Fine," I replied, thinking of what Hailey would say about that. *Freaked out, insecure, neurotic, emotional.*

"Good," he said. "Because I have a surprise for you."

My eyes narrowed. "What kind of surprise?"

"You'll see."

We got to Pickles for dinner and he ordered me my usual while I stood at the drink counter, twisting the paper off the straws and letting them fall like snow onto the counter top. I looked up to see him watching me, a grin spreading across his face when our eyes met.

It would be so easy, I thought. To leave this place forever. No Hailey, no Kellen. *No Mom.* The last thought sent a surge of shame through me. How many times had I wished she would just go away? When it came down to it could I really leave her?

I sat down with Dad, biting into the warm turkey sandwich. "So, I did some work today," he said. He rifled through his briefcase, pulling out a laptop and opening it to show me the screen. "There's this private school not far from Salina. They have the best swim team in the state. Two of their swimmers last year went on to swim at Division 1 schools." I leaned in at the picture of the team, red swimming suits, each of them holding up a trophy. He paused, studying my face. "They have try-outs coming up."

"When?"

"Next week."

My eyes rose, meeting his. "I called and they said they would let you try out even without formal training. The tuition isn't cheap but we'll make it. I just need you to say yes."

I looked down at the mac and cheese on my plate, at the pickle that tasted so good the first time he brought me here but now seemed rubbery and gross. The people around us were all talking, laughing. No one seemed to notice that my entire life was changing.

"What about Mom?"

I watched my dad's hands grip his coffee cup a little tighter. "Your mom took you away from me seven years ago," he said, struggling to keep his voice soft. "And I've missed you every day since then. You didn't have a

choice then, but you do now. Do you want to live your life like this, Ari?"
He paused, "That's your real name. Ari. Not Cass. Do you want to live in a
broken-down RV your whole life and work at the Waffle Stop? You could be
great at something. You could swim professionally."

"In a pool?" It was the first thing that came to mind. "There's no ocean
in Kansas."

He shook his head. "No, there's not."

"You just want me to leave with you? Without even talking to Mom?"

"Your Mom would be unhappy to see me here, Ari. She would be angry.
And she would not let you go. She's a controlling woman. She'll make you
stay even if you don't like it. Even if you're unhappy."

I bit a hangnail on my thumb, watching the blood pool along the nail
bed. "She'll convince you that living as a half-creature half-human—or
whatever she is—is the only way," he said, his voice lowering to almost a
whisper. "When being a part of *this* world, the real world is what matters.
You don't have to have that life, Ari. You can choose a new one."

"Half-creature," I said softly, my eyes rising to meet his. "Is that what
you think of me, too?"

His eyes sparked. "I didn't know you had . . . I wasn't sure . . ." He
paused, trying to control the smile that was filling his face—spreading
across his cheeks and raising them up to his eyes. "No. I think it's fine if you
can change and all that. But swimming around to boat wrecks? It's nuts. It's
unnecessary. That's what the coast guard is for. And those guys are actually
paid to do it." He swallowed, and I watched his Adam's apple bob along his
hairy neck. "You can have a different life, Cass. One that's all about you."

I felt tears spring to my eyes. He was right. It was kind of nuts. But
the look on that family's face when me and Mom got them all to shore was
amazing. It was the best thing I'd ever done. And Mom had done so many
more.

I stood up. "I gotta go."

"Wait, Ari—please talk to me. We can go today. We can leave this
place."

I ran to the door. "Ari!" he called after me, running to the cashier with
his wallet to pay the bill. "Hold up!"

But I was gone, racing with my backpack down the hill, my feet pounding on the pavement. Body carrying me towards the water.

Chapter Nineteen

I could swim faster than I could run. I threw the new shoes and the vest into my backpack and plunged into the water at the beach. It was murky here, dirty and washed up with leaves everywhere and the water felt cold and unfamiliar at first.

But the salt seeped into my skin and I paddled farther into the waves, closing my eyes as I transformed, the familiar tug and pull destroying the brand new leggings my Dad had just bought me. I didn't even care. Let them rip.

I felt the wind blow the waves closer to shore, and drowned out the noise from the city, the stillness of the ocean calming me. I paddled fast, zipping through the blue water. I had to get to Mom. I had to tell her everything all of a sudden, every secret I'd been building up felt ready to erupt.

"Mom!" I said, coming up the beach to the campground and pulling on the spare pair of spandex shorts I thought to bring from my soggy backpack. "Mom!"

I could see Hobs and his red hat from here. "Mom!"

I raced through the campground, ignoring the stares of tourists as I flung open the door. "Mom!"

She was sitting at the dinette working on a crossword puzzle. "Cass." She stood up. "Cass, what's wrong?"

I stood at the door, my hair and clothes dripping a puddle onto the ground.

"He's back, Mom." I hadn't realized I was crying until now. Something about the ocean seemed to absorb my tears, saltwater returning to its own.

"Who's back?" she asked, reaching for a towel and rubbing my back.

"Dad."

I told her how he showed up at work one day. About the hours at the restaurants, the shopping at the mall, his promise of a new life in Kansas. She listened without tears or anger, like her heart was absorbing the truth instead of her face.

When I told her about today, and his plea to leave, she put her head in her hands, her whole body slumping forward. "Cass, I'm so sorry," she finally said, rising up with tears in both eyes. "I'm so sorry for not telling you the whole truth. For feeling like you were too young for it."

I bit my lip. How could I have hidden him from her for so long? "Sit down, honey," she said. "It's time you learned the truth. All the truth."

I sat, curling my knees toward my chest, imagining his face today at Pickles, his arms around me yesterday when he told me he loved me. I couldn't understand why I felt so nervous when I'd been waiting for these answers my entire life.

"Before I begin, let me just say that there's a reason I've kept these things from you. And after you transformed and came to understand what a beautiful force of the sea you are, I knew we would need to have this conversation soon. But Cass." She paused, a tear forming in the corner of her eye. "I wish so much that I could shelter you from the truth forever."

I closed my eyes, pressing them tight together so that all of her words would just seep into my brain without me having to look at her face.

"I told you that your father and I both were in love with the sea," she said. I nodded through my closed eyes. "And I told you that he knew what I was, and at first, he was okay with all of it. Proud of it even."

I nodded again.

"But what I didn't tell you, is that he, well." She paused. "He's a scientist. Everything to him is facts and figures. And he had a lot of trouble with the idea of us keeping ourselves so hidden. He wanted us to be free to be who we are without hiding. But he didn't go about it in quite the right way."

"What did he want to do?"

"He wanted to learn about how the ocean called to us. Why it's only women who can transform. He had all these questions that he couldn't explain by science. And they started driving him crazy."

She paused. "But I loved him." Her eyes went glossy. "We were still happy together and I was willing to help him with his tests and his questions. "It was all fine. Great, actually, until we had you."

I looked down at the scratched dinette table. At the big dent from the time Mom put the hot pan on it and melted the plastic and tried not to think about me being born and ruining everything.

"I wanted to keep you from all of the testing he was doing," she said. "So you could discover who you were on your own. But he was so excited when you were a girl and wanted me to allow you to go to the lab with him. He wanted to see if things changed in your blood from birth, if you were different from other babies. And at first," she paused, "I let it happen because it seemed harmless enough. But as you began to get older . . ." Her mouth twisted. "It made me realize that he was not just curious."

"What do you mean?"

She shook her head, trying not to cry. "You came home from the lab one day and your hair was soaking wet."

"Yeah?" I asked, feeling a sudden tightening in my chest.

"I found out that he had shown you to a group of his colleagues. They were all involved in his research. And they wanted me to sign papers that would basically give you to the lab. You would become their project. Apparently they found something unique in your blood. The sodium was high I guess. Salt. I thought before then that it was just your father being curious. But he was using you to further his career. He wanted you to live permanently in the lab. He said it would be a wonderful opportunity."

I shifted as the pain in my chest widened. The tightening was getting worse and a shrill ring was sounding in my ear. It wouldn't stop it was so high, piercing, and bright. The lights above me began to flicker a bit. Or was it my eyes that were causing the light to flicker?

"He told me if I didn't sign the papers, he would out all of us. He would write to the papers and expose this whole society of rescuers. The Girls of the Ocean would all be in danger. And once that happened, well . . ."

Her voice continued, I was sure of it, but I could no longer hear her. A ringing in my ear kept me from hearing anything but the ocean outside, the lapping of the water onto the sand. It sounded almost violent from here. How had I never noticed that before?

"Cass, are you okay?" She was beside me now, her hand on my shoulder.

I shook my head, trying not to throw up. "I don't think so. I have this weird," and then a tug began, like a magnetic force, the ocean calling to me, screaming for me, pulling at me.

"Does it feel like your heart is going to come out of your mouth?" Mom asked, a smile crossing her face.

I swallowed, struggling to take deep breaths, heave in and out. "Yeah," I said. "I think I'm gonna be sick."

Her face went in and out of focus. "Honey, you're getting your first land call. This is how the ocean reaches you when you're not in it. This is a great thing. There's someone out there who needs you."

I gasped for air, thinking of her standing in the kitchen at the Waffle Stop all those days, her sudden exits that made me so mad. Was she in this much pain all those times?

"How come you're not getting it?" I asked. She was blinking her tears away. I could tell she was so happy for me and so sad at the same time.

"We don't all get the same calls," she explained. "There's not enough of us. So the ocean reaches out to us specifically for calls that are right for us. Sometimes it's because we have the right skills for that save. Sometimes it's because we're the closest rescuer. And sometimes," she sighed. "Sometimes the ocean calls us because we have something to learn."

"What do I do about them?" I asked, fighting back the pinching feeling in my heart with everything in me. I was already so exhausted, so overcome with emotion and fatigue. The last thing I wanted to do was go out now. It was already dark, a faint rim of dusky light through the tangled blinds of the dinette.

She was finally talking about my dad. She was finally telling me the truth. The ocean couldn't have chosen a worse time.

"You get in the water," she said softly. "And you answer their call."

Chapter Twenty

The water was cold in the dark, a chill running down my spine as I transformed easily for the second time that day and began to swim in the direction of the call. Any sleepiness I had before was gone now. I was all wire and momentum and energy. My first solo call. But I couldn't help but feel a little annoyed that it was happening just as my mom was beginning to tell me the truth.

Was it true that Dad wanted to treat me like another specimen in a jar? To do experiments? Was his curiosity greater than his love for me?

That thought made my stomach turn.

I soared through the waves like someone was trying to catch me, afraid that something was lurking in the water ready to snatch me. I knew that I could out swim whatever it was—shark, eel, jellyfish—but still, being in the ocean when it was this dark was frightening. Each wave held a deadly creature. Each swell would drag me under.

The tightening went away as soon as I transformed, but the cry of the ocean was louder than ever. Behind it there was a little bit of electricity too. Something buzzed in my ear. The current felt supercharged. I was following a pretty straight course near the land so the save couldn't be too deep.

The scream continued as I reached a little jetty—waves lapping up onto a rocky shelf. There was an overturned canoe up ahead, or at least I thought that was it. A long, narrow boat turned on its side was being tossed in the waves. But where were the people? And why wasn't it stopping as I neared like it had with the refugee save?

I plunged under, able to see, I discovered, in the water in the dark. It wasn't like a flashlight was shining on it the way it was lit up in movies. It was like a halo was cast over the entire ocean surrounding me. I saw fish darting back and forth like they did in the day. A rim of seaweed deeper below.

I shook my head, refocusing on the mission. There were people here, somewhere, there were people in the water who were struggling. I kicked harder, getting closer to the boat. But there was no movement around it, no people, but no waves either, no bubbles from lungs or arms flailing.

I frowned, wishing so badly that Mom was here. I thought of every question I should have asked her before. How to find the people who needed help. How to know if it was a save or a protection or a rescue. How to keep yourself hidden in the broad daylight. How to know when your mission is complete. And what if there were multiple missions at the same time? Which one did you choose?

I kicked closer to the overturned boat when I felt it. Something slipped around my fin so fast that I couldn't shake it before something tightened on my waist and a net rose over my whole body. Before I could think, I was picked up, unable to get free.

Flashes began as I was pulled to the surface, faces behind camera lenses, but I was transforming, changing so quickly that I didn't realize I had nothing on my bottom until I felt the harsh net on my bare skin. I pulled my T-shirt down, trying to cover myself as the net was placed on a boat, so many people talking at once that I didn't hear the sound of my own sobs until seconds later when a familiar voice spoke.

"Ari." Dad was untying the top of the net, and handed me a blanket to place over my shaking legs. I let him pull me out and wrap me up, a shiver going through my spine.

"Dad?" I asked through my sobs. "What are you doing here? Who are these people?"

The boat fell silent, the only sounds the waves lapping against the side of the boat. "This is my team," he said slowly. "I wanted to tell you everything before. How there was this big group here waiting to speak to you. But then you left, and I didn't get a chance. So I had to bring you here to show you myself. The amazing things you could do with us."

A girl, blonde with dark framed glasses reached out her hand. "Hi, I'm Nina. We've been waiting for a long time to finally meet you. That was," she took a deep breath, "Absolutely amazing. Your transformation was more beautiful than I could have ever guessed."

"You brought me here?" I asked him, pushing her hand away. "How? Why?" All of a sudden I missed my Mom so much I wanted to scream. She would never trap me. She would never use me this way.

"The ocean calls to you using hydroacoustics. It's similar to how whales communicate to each other. Using pulses and long drawn-out echoes. I learned years ago that it's how mermaids are drawn to the ocean for a save. A human's struggle sends out a pulse to the ocean, and it then reaches out to an individual equipped to answer the cries for help."

"So you . . ."

"Used your DNA in this machine that we built," he said with excitement. "It's used to draw those matching this code to the water, utilizing this sound. I can't believe it worked so well." He smiled with his hands on his hips, nodding around to all of these strangers.

I felt like I'd just been slapped in the face. These people were all staring at me and my dad—the man I thought was here to see me and get to know me the past couple weeks had just wanted one thing. To study me. To feed his curiosity.

"You're a monster."

"I'm your dad," he said softly, seeing the fear on my face. He turned to the others. "Give us a moment okay, guys?"

They turned their backs to us, but the boat was so small that they couldn't really get away. I could hear their murmurs and excited whispers anyway.

"Ari—Cass," he corrected. "I was going to tell you all of this. How once we got back to Salina you would have the chance to participate in ground-breaking research. You would be the world's first documented mermaid. Can you imagine? You'd have everything in life you could ever want. Stardom. Movies, a television show if you wanted it. You'd be on the covers of magazines and even more importantly—you'd make it possible for other mermaids to be free from hiding. People will love you."

"They'll destroy me!" I said, anger in the form of tears streaming down my face. "You think people will be okay with this? There's a reason we've been hiding for centuries!" I yelled. "We'll be put in tanks at aquariums! Or worse—in tanks in laboratories. We won't have a normal life! None of us will have a normal life!"

He frowned, "What's so great about a normal life?"

I stood up, trying not to let him notice as I edged toward the front of the boat. He grabbed my wrist. "Please cooperate, Ari. These people have been working your entire life on this project. Give them some credit for trying to discover more about what you are."

I tried to shake him off, "No!" I cried, "Let me go! I don't want this! I don't want to be in a tank! I don't want a television show!"

"You want to live in a camper and work as a waitress?" he shot back. "No daughter of mine will be doing that. You're a mermaid. Not a human. Accept that you are special!"

He waved at the bow of the boat where a guy with one of those dorky light headbands was standing. "Let's drive, Mike," he called. "Before her mom and her friends get any ideas."

I stomped on his foot, wrestling his arm away from me. "No! Get away!" The ocean was so close. I could transform. Outswim any speed boat. I could get Mom out. Hobs would loan us his truck. We could disappear again. This would be just another old life. I could have a new name. Choose any one I like. We could go to Hawaii. The Gulf. Alaska.

He twisted my arm and pulled me back by the neck of my T-shirt. "Get the net back!" he yelled, and Nina, the researcher with the glasses obeyed, slipping it over my body as I fought her.

"Stop!" I yelled. "Let me go!"

Dad knelt beside me as I fought, the boat speeding toward shore, so close to home. How long would it take before Mom came to look for me? Would she even know where to find me?

"I'm so sorry," he said, pulling out a syringe from what looked like a tackle box. "I hope you can forgive me for this," he said softly. "Because even though it may not seem like it right now, I really do love you very much."

I watched him in horror, the particles of air around us seeming to slow with the ripple of the water. I think I tried to yank back my arm, but he was holding me so tight that the cold needle pierced my arm, a shoot of pain racing through my bloodstream. Meanwhile, the moon watched, soft bands of water shaking the circle of white.

I felt myself get tired suddenly, my limbs loose and heavy.

The waves beat against the boat. They would free me, wouldn't they? I was a Girl of the Ocean. I was—

But darkness found me first. And for the first time in my life, I thought that this must be what drowning feels like. Limbs that won't move, sputtering lungs, and then darkness.

Chapter Twenty-One

"Good morning."

My eyelids fluttered as I struggled to open them, gravity too much to handle right now. White light—bright and strange surrounded me. Like every surface was reflecting the glow of the bulbs.

My eyes drifted from the white light down to the bed I was in. I held my hands to my face, palms turned to inspect them. If this was not real, then neither was I. I was still lost in a dream. The heaviest, most frightening dream I could imagine.

"How are you feeling?"

I traced the light to meet the voice. A gray-flecked beard smiled at me, two watery blue eyes grinning above it. "You were out for awhile. I apologize for that. But I had to make sure you wouldn't fight us." He paused. "Did you know that rabbit mothers leave their burrow after giving birth? They only stop by a few minutes a day afterwards to feed the litter. And less than a month later, the baby rabbits are left to fend for themselves. Do you know why?"

I swallowed, feeling a throb in my head I hadn't noticed until then. My entire body was waking up.

"The rabbit mother is actually helping her babies. By avoiding them, she is minimizing the chance that the rabbit burrow will be found by predators."

He grinned. "I am the rabbit mother. I left you alone for awhile—with your mom in St. Augustine, Florida—keeping away the predators. I let you live that sad life to protect you until you, and we—were ready."

"Where am I?" I asked, my tongue so heavy I could barely move it to make the words.

"You're in a laboratory near Boston, Massachusetts." He straightened. "And I am thrilled to have you here at last."

All of a sudden it was as though my brain was kicked into gear, a slow melt from its cold winter state. Like me finally being able to tell Kellen I liked him times ten. I remembered everything. The weeks my dad spent with me, picking me up from school, buying me Pickles and watching my swim meets. The day he asked me to move in with him. And then the night—that terrible night on the boat. The feeling of the rough net around my skin, the flashes and the people and the ocean waves beating against us.

"I thought you lived in Salina, Kansas."

"I did! For a few years after you disappeared. But then this lab gave me funding and the team moved out here."

I squinted into the light. "You said you played basketball with Danny. You told me you did triathlons. Taught at a school there." I couldn't for the life of me think of the name of it.

"Well," he said after a long pause, "Those were half-truths, I guess. Things I wished would happen. Things that maybe could have happened if you had stayed out there with me."

"I'm thirsty," I said, because I couldn't make myself say what I wanted to say.

He bolted up. "Let me get you something."

I watched him pull a plastic container from a white shelf and fill it at a tap. He then placed it on a table, closing one eye to look at how much was in it and then handed it to me.

I took it warily. "Did you put something in this?"

He shook his head with a grin. "Of course not! I just wanted to note how much you were offered, and how much you drank. We will also be measuring your output. Nothing to be embarrassed about."

"You're going to measure how much I pee?"

"That's one way of putting it."

Tears pricked my eyes, and when I closed them tightly, trying to close out the light, I felt them fall onto my cheeks, my sudden fear and sadness so strong I ached to be in the water.

"How could you," I whispered.

His hand reached for mine, squeezing it so tight I knew that no matter how hard I tried I wouldn't be able to free myself of it. So I didn't try. I let him hold it.

"I'm sorry. But everything I am doing, everything I have done is out of love for you."

"Love shouldn't be so heavy," I heard myself say. Something I remember Mom saying what felt like years ago as we sat, bobbing in the water in our sea.

My days began and ended the same. Dad showed up to bring me breakfast and dinner. Usually some kind of eggs or meat with a salad. We sat in silence as I picked at my food, and he asked me questions about my life at home while I ignored him. He watched me carefully, pausing to take notes on his tablet when I wasn't looking, and always checking the toilet—part of a closet built into the room for my "output." During the days, he disappeared for long stretches of time and Nina came.

I recognized her from the boat. Late twenties, shoulder-length blonde hair, black-framed glasses, and a scent of Chapstick floating around her at all times. Probably because she pulled it out every ten minutes to apply more.

For a couple days all she did is sit with me. We didn't leave the room. She brought books and a small television. I pretended like she wasn't there. I ignored her questions.

Every so often she got a phone call, from my dad no doubt, and left the room. I watched her pace back and forth outside the room from the small window cut into the door, watching me watch her.

My dad asked me questions in the evenings. What did I do today? Did I enjoy Nina's company? What book was I reading?

But I was silent, fear striking me every time I really considered what was happening. I had been kidnapped by my own father. He tricked me into thinking he loved me. I let him feed me. I let him pick me up from school and watch me swim and all that time he was priming me for his own experiments.

Silence felt like the only way I could punish him.

On day three—or was it four?—my dad came in the morning and did not leave. I watched him make notes on his tablet and picked at my dry toast, missing Mom more than I could imagine missing anyone or anything. She loved me. How could I have lied to her? How could I have trusted this stranger more than her?

"All right," he said when he finished, "I helped you escape your life. Now I need your help."

I shook my head.

"Ari, please," he said.

My name is Cass. I considered breaking the silence for a moment but decided not to. Silence was the only weapon I had left.

Lines hardened around his eyes. "You'll come with me. We have investors coming. We've talked about this for years and they've graciously funded me based on the evidence I've shown them. Bringing you here was a way to keep them interested in funding our lab. And if they can see what you can really do, they will also get you in touch with some powerful people. We're talking big money, Ari. Roles in movies. A reality television show. Anything you want. Magazine covers," he added hopefully.

I blinked at him like I didn't care at all about what he was saying, but inside I felt screams shuttle up and down my spine. *Someone, anyone please help me,* I begged. If I transform, if my body showed these "investors" what it could do, I would be trapped here forever. He would never let me out of this prison.

Nina came to the door. "Hey Ari," she said. "You ready for this?" With one hand she pulled me up, leading me down a white hallway, the air cold and sterile. There were so many doors in this hall that I wondered for a minute how many other people they had trapped in there, but then I realized that I was probably the only one. The only rescuer or Girl of the Ocean or whatever we were that was dumb enough to get caught.

Finally, we reached a tall metal door. "This is the one!" My dad scanned a badge on the door and we stepped into a dimly lit warehouse, walls from ceiling to floor filled with odds and ends—dangling cords, tall glass cylinders, old chemistry equipment spilling from brown boxes. But in the center rested a giant tank, stretching almost from end to end, half-filled with saltwater.

The water called to me. The closer I got to the tank, the more my nerves began to twitch. I felt my hands begin to tingle, my heart rate speeding up.

"It's calling to you, isn't it?" He gripped my wrist, feeling my pulse, then nodded at Nina. "She's responding to it. Our hypothesis is correct. We have purposefully kept you away from the water for several days. Nothing in your food or your water has been touched by salt. But this water was pulled directly from the ocean—it's seawater. And your body is hungry for it. Which means that the longer mermaids are kept from the water, the more intense their cravings get."

I frowned. I had lived most of my life by the ocean, and the pull to the water had never been this strong.

"You may not have had these cravings before, because living near the ocean, your body had a daily dose of saltwater from the air you breathe. That's why most mermaids choose to live by the ocean," my dad explained, like he could read my mind.

He pointed to the tank. "The investors will be arriving soon. All I need you to do is transform one time. Real quick and swim a couple laps and then you are free to go back to your room and watch America's Next Top Model for the rest of the day. How is that? I'll even see if Nina can find you a warm turkey sandwich like we had at Pickles. Maybe a chocolate chip cookie, too?"

My stomach churned at the mention of the food since I had barely eaten a thing since arriving there. But more than that, I felt my fear heighten. I had such little control over my transformations as it was, and the pull to the water was so real. Still, I could not let these outsiders see. I would put myself, my mom—all of the Girls of the Ocean—at risk.

Nina gestured for my dad to turn around so she could help me pull off my leggings.

"No!" I shouted, breaking the silence for the first time as she and my dad carried me, fighting as hard as I could, towards the tank. "I won't do it! No! Stop it! Please!"

I felt tears fall down my face as they pulled me toward the tank. My dad yanked my arm towards him, forcing me into a tight hold, the muscles from his triathlon more pronounced than they look on him. He was so much stronger than me. "Stop! Please stop!"

With a grunt, he pushed me up the ladder. "It will be over before you know it. Just show us one time and you can go back. Won't that be nice? Just one time, Ari, and your whole life will change!"

"*No!*" I screamed as he held me over the ledge, throwing me into the tank where I fell several feet before I hit the water. A door slid on the top of the tank to trap me in.

My tears fell, mixing with the water that had wrapped me up inside of it, soothing me in its wake.

I could see him through the glass, and suddenly, I could hear him—his voice amplified by a speaker in the tank. "Ari, can you hear me? I'm about to let them in. Just one time. Just once and it will all be over. You can do this. I love you, sweetheart. I love you so much."

I closed my eyes, letting myself float in the water, doing everything I possibly could not to transform, even though my limbs ached to change and my legs were twitching in the water. My heart was beating so fast it felt like it would burst. To block out the pain from not transforming, I imagined Mom and Hailey at home, missing me. I thought about the safety of our little camper and Hobs and even Shara and the Waffle Stop.

"I will not change," I said out loud into the water. "I am not Ari, I am Cass."

I turned to the people behind the glass, six men and two women, all of them dressed in black, their faces watching me curiously as I swam. "I'm a prisoner!" I yelled, pounding on the glass. "Help me! Help me!"

But instead of helping me, they watched me. They made notes on their tablets. My dad pled, begging me through the speaker to show them what I could do.

But I fought the urges inside of me with every ounce of power I had. I would not transform for him. I would not transform for them.

That power belonged only to me.

Chapter Twenty-Two

"Please eat something."

I stared at the two fried eggs on my plate, a mound of grapes and a croissant next to them. "We need you to keep your strength up," my dad added, eyeing the chart on his tablet.

I knew what it said. That I wasn't eating enough. That my "output" wasn't healthy. It had been two days since he asked me to change in front of his investors. Afterwards he was so angry with me, he asked Nina to escort me back to my room and didn't come to visit me for a full 24 hours. When he finally did, he apologized, saying, "Of course you weren't ready," and, "What was I thinking?" But then he told me they were coming back in three days and they were growing impatient, and did I really not care at all about my future? About his?

To pass the time, and to keep myself from thinking about the tank of saltwater just down the hall, I told myself the stories Mom told me about her time as a Girl of the Ocean.

"Once I went on a call and there was nothing there. No sign of a wreck. Nothing but the waves and the stars above me. I sat in the middle of the water and waited. The call didn't go away so I didn't dare leave.

"A ripple came towards me. Slow at first and then faster and before I could swim away another Girl of the Ocean rose out of the water. Her

fin was almost black, and she wore a ratty Minnesota Vikings jersey on top. Her hair was short and white, her skin so wrinkled that it looked like she had spent her entire life in the water."

"Who was she?" I asked.

It was just weeks ago but felt like years. I felt a tear slide down my face at the thought of my mom, out there somewhere, looking everywhere for me. What if she found the note, crumpled in my new pair of jeans? What if she actually believed that I left her to live with my dad?

"She was a Girl, just like you and me. But she had seen a lot. I asked her if she needed help, but she shook her head with a grin and said, 'Baby—I'm stronger than a bull shark. I came out here to help you.'

"It was right after we left your dad. I was afraid to live alone. We had no money for food or rent. I was worried that any minute the feds would show up and take you away from me. I cried so much those first few months that I felt thirsty all the time. My body wrung itself dry.

"She took me by the hand. We swam together. She did not ask me to speak. She only swam with me. It was starting to get dark and I was worried about getting home to you and she told me before I left, 'Honey, we're everywhere. Every state, every continent, every island. I used to worry we'd all go extinct one day, but you know what? The older I get the more I think that we're all going to be okay. We'll help each other. We'll survive.' And then she pointed down into the water and said, 'Swim down. There's something of value below.' Then she swam away."

"What was it? A chest of treasure?" I asked sarcastically. Mom's stories were usually exciting. They went somewhere. She saved people.

"I swam below. It was getting dark. But deep under the surface, nearly covered by a massive piece of coral, I found a clamshell with the most perfect wild pearl you'll ever see. I took it to a nearby jeweler, and that is how we lived for the first year until I finally got a job as a fry cook at Rosita's."

"Our girls are everywhere," she said. *"Everywhere you can imagine."*

"I don't know how to emphasize how important today is," Dad said. "They may not give me another chance. If you love me at all, do this one thing. Change. Just once. You can even stay as a mermaid if you'd like after so you don't have to worry about the modesty factor."

All morning he spoke to me, fear in his milky eyes. "And please, for the love, Ari, just eat something. Anything."

Two Eggo waffles sat on my plate, doused in syrup, the scent making me throw up a little in my mouth every time I caught a whiff.

"Can you commit to doing this?" he reached for my hand, grasping it in his tightly. A cage around me, too strong to break through. His grip got tighter. "Say you will."

I stared at him, unflinching.

He sighed. "I didn't want it to come to this, but you've left me no choice."

He waved Nina over, who stood by the door, rushing forward when he motioned to her. "Get the footage."

They placed a tablet in front of me, a crackle of black and white, and then—a large tank, not unlike the one they placed me in before. Everything looked dark, like a filter was placed over the footage. Her long green fin ruffled beneath her as she swam, back and forth in the water. Turning suddenly to the camera, her face coming into view.

"*Mom!*" I yelled. I watched her long hair dragging behind her. "*No! Mom! No!*" Nina took the screen abruptly, and my dad attempted to hug me, to pull me to him but it was so smothering, so sick and smothering that I could do nothing but sob.

"We got her days ago. She wants to see you. We'll bring you together again if you just change. I promise. No one will hurt you. But if you don't do it, you'll have left us no choice but to harm her. I'm sorry, Ari. It's the only way."

Tears fell from my face as they helped me up, my dad nearly carrying me out the door and down the hall. "I'm so sorry," he kept whispering to me, his breath tickling my ear.

"I hate you," I said. "I hate you, and I hate maple syrup. If you knew me, if you loved me at all, you would know that."

He blinked twice. "Everyone loves maple syrup."

Four men and two women sat on metal chairs near the front of the tank. My dad left my side and rushed toward them, shaking their hands one at a time, nodding and laughing while Nina stood near me with her arms crossed.

"Just do it once," she said without looking at me. "One time."

The water called to me, sweat forming on my palms and underarms. I felt thirsty for it, wanting so badly to be near it. I could feel my legs quiver beneath me.

"Ari, sweetheart, I'd like you to meet these lovely folks," my dad said suddenly, waving me forward.

Nina nudged me, a grin plastered beneath her layer of Chapstick. I shook the hands of two fat men, both of their jackets bulging beneath their coats. A short man with gray sideburns held my hand in his and pumped it enthusiastically before I was introduced to Ms. Maria Whitebart.

"Now Ari, this woman is our best benefactor. She has been sponsoring my research for years. In fact, she was my first investor. The first to believe what you are capable of."

He looked at me proudly, shooting looks between myself and Ms. Whitebart.

She was older, with short brown hair neatly curled and soft pink lips. Her white suit skimmed black high heels, and neatly stacked rows of diamond bracelets fell to her wrist. "Hello Ari," she said, meeting my eye. "I've waited for such a long time to meet you."

She lifted her hand for a moment, revealing a tattoo on her wrist. It was a blue dolphin, rising out of water, drops coming off of it. I stared at it for a moment, intrigued, until I caught a glimpse of my dad, grinning like a puppy at Ms. Whitebart, his goofy smile so embarrassing and gross that I turned back to her, and spat on the ground.

"Ari!" he exclaimed, grabbing me by the wrist. "That is very rude!"

He turned quickly to Ms. Whitebart and the other investors while squeezing my wrist firmly, "I'm so sorry for her behavior. She was raised by her mother entirely. I have no idea the kinds of manners she was taught, but as you can see . . ." He waved his free hand around and the investors all laughed politely—except for Ms. Whitebart. Her eyes stayed focused on mine, so locked in place that I felt like she was speaking to me in a language I could not understand.

Dad pulled on me, "Let's show them what they came here for, shall we?" he said, leading me toward the tank. Once on the other side he hissed,

"Don't forget about your mother. We have her and we will keep her as long as we have to to get you to change."

Nerves rained down as I stood behind the tank. I could see the tapping feet of the investors through it, bobbing up and down. The salt water pulled me, almost begging me to come in. I wondered if I would have any control once inside. Last time it took all of my strength to keep myself from transforming. Could I be that strong again? For my mom? For the other Girls of the Ocean?

Nina helped me pull off my robe, leaving me in a white cotton T-shirt and a pair of underwear. Then she motioned to the ladder at the base of the tank. "Go ahead."

I took a couple steps up, gripping the rails so tightly my whole hand was white. "I love you, Ari," my dad called to me at the base of the ladder. "I'm so proud of you. You're so brave. You're so strong."

I stood at the top, the water so enticing, the smell of salt wafting through my senses. For a second I thought of Hailey and her YouTube channel. Kellen and his swim meets. They were both in school right now, probably texting their friends, both glad to be rid of me. I envied them, not because of their normal lives, and their cell phones, and their parents that were still married for once, but because they were free.

"Go on, Ari!" my dad called, his arms crossed nervously as he stood by the investors. "You're safe here. You're in good company!"

My legs shook as I stood at the top of the tank. I scanned the faces of the investors, my eyes resting on Ms. Whitebart, who, right before the lights went out, held a finger to her lips and smiled.

Chapter Twenty-Three

There were no screams, unless you count my own. But when the lights flickered back on less than two minutes later, Nina laid at the base of the ladder, and my dad and all of the investors were on the floor too.

Ms. Whitebart stood at the base, extending her hand to me. "Hey Cass, doll. Let's get you home."

I stood with my back against the ladder now, looking down at this stranger, relief suddenly washing through me. "Who are you?" I asked.

"I'm a Girl of the Ocean, just like you and your mom." She extended her hand. "Now we better hurry because they won't stay like this for long and we've got a long way to go."

I scuttled down the ladder as Ms. Whitebart strolled past Nina, who lay open mouthed on the floor. She pulled a pair of gray sweatpants from her white leather handbag. "Here, put these on."

I took them from her. "Are they . . . Are they okay?"

"Yes, nothing serious. They'll wake up in about half an hour a little confused but with no permanent harm done."

"What did you do?" I paused to look at my dad, his arms spread out like a starfish across the cement floor.

"Same thing we do with people we save," she said. "It's the mermaid's kiss of death." She laughed. "It's how we get people to forget they saw us when they do a save. You'll learn all about it when you get some formal training. But that guy?" she pointed to my dad. "I gave him a solid twenty-five years of forgetting." She looked at me, as if to check that it was okay.

I thought of the time I spent with my dad the past few weeks. He wouldn't remember any of it. He wouldn't remember that he had a daughter at all.

Maybe that was the best thing.

"Now let's get out of this dump." She walked down the hall briskly, making a turn and pushing open a metal door.

"Sorry, but even twenty-five years of forgetting won't make him forget," I said. "He's been studying me and you, and our DNA with his team. He probably has tons of documents and research. Who knows."

She smiled. "After tonight, they'll think they were studying the mating patterns of jellyfish. My team helped create all new research, and they are, at this moment, uploading it onto all servers."

We stepped outside into a brisk spring morning. Trees grew outside the gray office building we just exited, birds swooping across a lush, green courtyard. "It's beautiful here." I blinked, feeling raw and strange. Like I had just been born.

"I own the place," Ms. Whitebart said. "I house several of my investments at this property, so when I came across an ambitious mermaid researcher out of Salina, Kansas, I insisted he must come and study them here in my space free of charge." She giggled like a little girl, pulling out a cell phone and rapidly punching in a number with her manicured hand.

"You're a genius."

"No, just a very rich Girl of the Ocean who fiercely desires to protect her friends." She paused. "Alexi? I have my darling with me, and we're ready for pickup. Thank you. See you soon."

We walked quickly across the green courtyard, rows of window-paned office buildings leading to a large parking lot. I took a deep breath, shocked at how quickly things had gone from terrible to *this*.

She greeted her driver at the foot of a large white SUV and waved me forward. "Let's get you home."

"*Wait!*" I said, suddenly realizing that my mom was still in there. How could I have forgotten about her? "My mom! She's still in there!" I started to run back to the gray building, my bare feet thumping against the cement painfully. "I can't leave her behind! Who knows what he'll do?"

"Cass!" Ms. Whitebart wobbled after me, struggling to keep up in her heels. "Your mother is fine! Your father used old footage to scare you!"

"How do you know?" I turned around, tears streaming down my face. "He showed me a video of her! He has her trapped! We have to save her too!" I pointed to the building. "She's in there!"

"Oh Cass," Ms. Whitebart said with a pursed smile. "I wanted it to be a surprise but, Alexi? Let out the fish."

The driver nodded and opened the car door.

My mom stepped out of the car then. Long hair braided with a piece of purple silk, oversized capris, and that white T-shirt with a mushroom on it. Definitely, unmistakably her.

"Oh Cass," she said as I ran to her, my tears falling so fast now I felt a shiver race down my back from the salt water. She wrapped me up in her arms, pulling my head to her and we both cried. "You're safe, you're safe," she kept repeating.

I glanced at Ms. Whitebart who was watching it all with a grin. "Okay you two, you have plenty of time to catch up on the flight home. I had plans to visit Tokyo this week for a merger but this took priority, so my plane is free. Now I need to get back inside before they all wake up and pretend like a robber attempted to steal all of our research on jellyfish. Should be the role of a century."

Alexi stifled a laugh behind a fisted hand.

"We owe you so much," my mom said, snot running across her upper lip.

"Nah," Ms. Whitebart said, already walking toward the gray building. "We're all on the same team here. I just spend more time saving on the land so you can put in your time saving in the water, that's all. Happy to help!"

She blew kisses at us as she walked away, her phone already to her ear.

Safe inside the car, huddled together with our hands clasped, my mom kissed my cheek and I nestled my head onto her shoulder. "Dad had this video of you, Mom. You had changed. I was so scared."

She rolled her eyes. "That was years ago. Before you were born! He told me he destroyed it but must have lied. I was worried sick about you for probably two hours, until Ms. Whitebart called Hobs. I don't know how that woman does it. She's not a fish. She's an angel!"

Alexi chuckled in the front seat, his hand positioned on the steering wheel. "Ladies, where to?"

I looked up at my mom. "We could go anywhere," she said. "There's nothing to keep us in St. Auggy. Is there anywhere you want to go? Any place you'd like to live and start over?"

I thought for a second as Alexi started the car, guiding us out of the parking lot. Wasn't it a fresh start that I wanted when I decided to move with Dad? A new place, new friends, a new school?

"I just want to go home," I said, surprising myself. "I want our beach and our camper."

"St. Augustine, Florida," Mom said to Alexi proudly, wrapping her arm around my shoulder. "To the ocean." He nodded and pushed a button, leaving a layer of glass between us.

We sat in silence as Alexi drove us through city traffic, and I felt more peaceful than I ever had before. Our secret was safe. I was free from my dad. And for once, I knew the truth about why we left. Mom was protecting me from him all along.

"Thanks for saving me, Mom," I whispered.

"No, thank you," she whispered, her lips on my head, kissing me over and over. "Thank you for saving me thirteen years ago. Thank you for saving me every day since."

Epilogue

"**A** little to the right, Cass! Yeah. Stop there. Right there."
I looked through the viewfinder. "It looks pretty good. But I gotta go after this one."

"'Kay, I'm ready." Hailey smoothed down her leotard, her feet turned out, the toe arched at an impossible angle.

"Welcome!" she exclaimed when she saw the red dot appear on the camera. "To Bal-ays, with Haize! I'm going to teach you little freaks how to do what is called a plié. With your feet out and heels planted on the ground, you're going to bend here at the waist. And I don't want to see *any* butts out of line! Keep them in tight!" she straightened her own back. "And, dip, and dip, and now with the arms . . ."

I stared out of the window of the ballet studio where we film, daylight disappearing behind the fallen clouds. It would be night soon, and I still had homework and a call with Ms. Whitebart and I really wanted to fit a swim in there too somehow. Mom trained me every chance she got and it was our nightly ritual to go out in the water.

Hailey finished dancing and curtsied. "Thank you! That's all for today! Make sure to subscribe to my channel below!"

I flipped the switch off. "Awesome."

She squealed, jumping in the air. "We're at over 5,000 subscribers already! Who knew all of those little girls and sad moms with no lives would want to learn ballet basics online? Not me." She reached for her backpack. "Did you hear that Kellen has a girlfriend?"

I let her help me stand up. "No. Who is it?"

"McKell from swim, I guess. The short one with the curly blonde hair."

I smiled. "Oh yeah, I know her. She's pretty cool."

"You don't care?" she pushed open the door.

"I don't," I said, surprising myself by feeling nothing when she said that.

"Good," Hailey said. "I was worried we would have to have a sleepover tonight and pig out on licorice and pizza and watch YouTube all night. But we could do that anyway?"

I laughed. "It's a school night, Haiz. I have homework. And a call with Maria."

"Oh yeah—your strange rich friend from Boston who mysteriously gives a girl who lives in a *camper* a job. Nothing weird about that. What do you do for her again?"

"I'm just helping her with some research," I said. "She's really into fish."

Maria Whitebart contacted me and my mom less than a week after we took her private jet back to St. Auggy and offered us both a job. I would be her researcher, digging up anything the internet had to say about Girls of the Ocean and cataloging them. And Mom, well, she was hired to help Maria write a book. Documenting saves, getting stories from other Girls of the Ocean, and providing tips and tactics to remain unseen. "It's time we started keeping track of the good we're doing," Maria had said. She was paying us more a week than we both made a month at The Waffle Stop. And best of all, the hours were flexible so Mom could focus on saving as much as she wanted.

It didn't hurt that she got us a cell phone to share that my mom let me keep.

Hailey wrapped her arm around my waist. "Thanks for helping me today, Cass. You're the best."

"No problem!" I said, already heading for the water.

"Are you sure you don't want a ride, you maniac?" she called after me.

"Nah," I said. "You know I'd rather swim."

I walked down to the beach, waving at an older couple taking a stroll across the sand. Some teenagers were kissing on a blanket. I pulled my shoes off, tucked my things in my backpack and started wading into the water.

The moon reflected across every point of the water, each wave crashing to destroy it before it appeared again, persistent and bright.

"Is it always this hard?" I had asked my mom, days after we got back.

Hailey barely knew I was gone, Kellen only talked to me about swimming, and I was back at school in my same weird clothes. But then Maria visited the camper and everything changed, but some days? It was still hard. Hard being a Girl of the Ocean. Hard being a girl of the land.

"For a long time," Mom said. "But it's hard when you're all on land or all in water. It's hard for everyone. But it gets better." She rested her head on mine. "And the best part is? When life on land gets hard for you—you have somewhere to run."

I plunged into the water then, feeling my body change as I rose. I swam, flying through the sea, my backpack knocking against the back of my fin as I pushed faster, harder, eager to get home and tell Mom about my day. She would want to hear everything.

The water surged around me, following my every movement. I dove deep, as deep as I wanted, then raised my arms in a surge, water bursting past me as I came to the top. And just then, under a canopy of moon and salt, I felt vast, brilliant, strong. The feeling would come and go, but right in that moment—I was not a drop. I was not even a river.

I was the whole sea.

About the Author

Mandy M. Voisin graduated from Brigham Young University with a BA in English. She has lived in Arizona, Florida, and currently resides in Utah with her husband Kevin and her four children.

Girls of the Ocean is her second published novel. Check out her first, *Star of Deliverance,* and visit her website mmvoisin.com for more of her work.

Scan to visit

mmvoisin.com